the atonement

JUSTIFIED

BOOK THREE

STELLA JACKSON

Syncterface Media
London
www.syncterfacemedia.com

JUSTIFIED
ISBN: 978-1-912896-04-2
Copyright © July 2020
Stella Jackson
All Rights Reserved

Published in the United Kingdom by

Syncterface Media
London
www.syncterfacemedia.com
info@syncterfacemedia.com

Cover Design
Syncterface Media, London

This book is printed on acid-free paper

To the emotionally, physically,
mentally and sexually abused without a voice
without a voice:
Weeping may endure for a night,
But joy will come in the morning.

Foreword

I had just arrived home from the funeral of a young man who was a real role model for my children. I was heavy with raw emotion and still questioning the injustices of life when my phone rang. I listened, and while saying very little, I somehow agreed to write a foreword.

How was I going to read a book and articulate my synopsis when I was still so numbed by the unjustified loss of such a treasured young man?

The next day the manuscript arrived; the title: 'Justified'. I began to read and was gripped from the first page.

As I turned each page, I became more invested, provoked by the plot that was unfolding. How could anyone inflict such terrible acts upon another. I wanted justice for this dear child that had endured the unthinkable, and I needed to know the outcome. This novel took me on a journey with Leah and her mother during their darkest hours, but when many would have crumbled, they remained focused on what mattered the most.

The plot progresses through this book in such a way that each page hooks you in just a little bit further. Before I could find the right place to pause and put the book down I had reached the end.

I have known Stella for many years, and she has been one of those precious people who I cherish as a dear friend and a real powerhouse. A pillar of light and encouragement to me, my children, my family and the community. Stella has an unwavering passion, determination and commitment to improving the world. Everyone who has had the pleasure of knowing Stella will testify, they are enhanced by her presence in their lives, no matter how brief.

I feel truly honoured to write this foreword, and I am thankful for the timely opportunity to let in some light when I needed it the most, reminding me where my focus needs to be.

~ **Clare Elevique** ~
Communications Business Partner, IC Practitioner & Mentor

1

DECISIONS

It dawned on Michael Doland that he had come to the end of the road. The harsh reality of his sins was staring him straight in the face; he could no longer run from the wrong he had done. He had learnt of Josie Kimberley's return from her self-imposed exile and her determined intention to seek justice against him in a court of law, but what bothered him the most was his father's plan to wash his hands off him. Michael knew that without his father, his case was as good as lost.

Before he and his wife were confronted by their daughters Winifred and Jennifer, Sir Ian had made up his mind to do the right thing. The victims deserved justice, and he was determined to do all within his power to ensure that they got it. Lady Donna, on the other hand, planned to back her son to the very end. She was opposed to an out of court settlement and made it clear that if Josie wanted a legal battle, then so be it.

This bothered Ian as he wondered how his wife could assume that their son would win the case if it went to court, especially after everything he had heard. He had been reliably informed that his son's case file had been sent to the Crown Prosecution Office and assigned to a judge. The only thing he wasn't sure about was whether it was going to be judge and jury or not, but if he were to advise the Kimberleys, he would definitely request a jury.

"Well, the chicken has come home to roost," Sir Ian soliloquised.

Deep down, he knew he couldn't lay all the blame on Donna. After all, he was very much aware of his son's weaknesses; lying and making up silly excuses to cover his antics, never taking responsibility for his actions, and of course, his inability to resist any moving object in a skirt. Even though Michael was able to get away with all his shenanigans thanks to his mother, Ian knew that if he had put his foot down instead of using the weather as an excuse to run off to New Zealand, he just might have been able to keep their son in check.

He knew that his wife would do anything to protect their son, so it really shouldn't have come as a surprise when she hinted at him using his influence to pervert the course of justice, but it did! He had planned not to get involved, but now he found himself reminiscing. He didn't want to let his daughters down, and he believed that justice should be served, but at the same time, he didn't want to ostracise his wife or his son for that matter. He was still in deep thought when his phone rang.

"Hello," Ian answered, not looking at the caller display.
"Hello Sir Ian, it's Father O'Connor."
"Oh, hello Father. To what do I owe the pleasure of this call?"
"Well, I was wondering if we could meet up sometime in the evening to discuss a few things. It is quite urgent."
"That should be fine. Do you want me to come over to the Presbytery, or would you rather we meet at the coffee shop? I am available any time after five o'clock if that helps."

"Lovely. In that case, let us meet at the Presbytery," Father O'Connor replied. "I have to visit a sick parishioner at two, but I should be back before five, and in case I'm not, I'll instruct Mr Coleman, the housekeeper, to take good care of you."

"Alright Father, see you at five then."

"What could be so urgent?" Ian wondered as he paced the room nervously. He mused that it could have something to do with the upcoming court case, but even though Father O'Connor was a close friend and confidant, what was he supposed to tell him? He was still pacing up and down when he heard the front door open. It was his wife.

"Welcome back, dear," he enthused. "I hope you had a nice time with your friends?"

Lady Donna, ignoring her husband's pleasantries, unleashed what was on her mind.

"Ian, I have heard rumours. It seems the Kimberleys, despite their promise not to press charges, are instigating the police and the Crown Prosecution Service to take the alleged rape of their daughter to court. Well, if they want war, then so be it! You have got to speak to Charles Quinn, the QC who handled the Muswell case two years ago."
"Donna, please sit down," Ian said in a firm, quiet voice.

She was about to argue when Sir Ian placed a finger on his lips, signalling to her to keep quiet.

"Donna, listen to yourself. Is it really that hard to have the milk of human kindness towards Josie and Leah? Not once have I heard you ask after the little girl nor taken out time to actually try and find out what transpired between Michael and his daughter."

"But, Ian…"

"Please, let me finish," he thundered.

Lady Donna was frightened as her husband's tone brought back memories of when she did not want to relocate to London with him after giving birth to Michael.

"I will not be part of a conspiracy to pervert the course of justice. Allow the court to do its job. If our son is found guilty, then he must face the consequences of his crime."

"Ian, you disappoint me!" she exclaimed. "For someone who was on the bench for so long, it is a shame to see that you have already judged and condemned your son without hearing his side of the argument. Michael said that it was consensual and I believe him. With or without you, I intend to secure the services of Mr Quinn to lead a team of defence lawyers to prove my son's innocence."

"Is that meant to be a threat?" Sir Ian asked. "Donna, I strongly advise you not to waste time and money. The law on rape cases has tightened significantly, and I can assure you that if Michael faces a jury, he will be found guilty and he will serve time."

Without uttering another word, Sir Ian left the room glancing at his watch.

Lady Donna knew that her husband was right, and without him she was fighting a lost cause.

"If only my father were still here," she thought.

Lady Donna's father had always been her rock and spoiler; the one she could always rely on to do anything she wanted. But with him gone, she found herself with no one to fall back on. Her mother was still alive, but they never really got along. Besides, the old woman had retired to her seaside cottage in Cornwall, and she knew there was no way her mother would get involved with anything concerning Michael.

The Presbytery was only a few miles away, but as Sir Ian sat in the back seat of his chauffeur-driven car taking in the refreshing atmosphere of the countryside, he couldn't help but think about the shame and pain that Michael had brought upon them over the years. If Michael's case were to go to trial, all their dirty linen would most likely be exposed during the interrogations. Was he prepared for the stain this would bring to the family name? Maybe he should approach the Kimberleys and plead with them to drop the case, but would he do that if Josie was his own daughter? And what about little Leah? How could a father rape both mother and child? Sir Ian hung his head in shame.

As they drove into the church courtyard, he was still lost in thought, and when the driver came round to open the door, Sir Ian found himself momentarily disoriented and at a loss as to why he was there in the first place. However, it all came back to him when he saw a smiling Father O'Connor waving from afar.

"Hello Sir Ian," the Padre began. "Good to see you. Is it okay if we go to my study?"
"That is fine by me," Sir Ian replied.

Both men made their way into the house, and as they sat down, the Padre asked his guest if he would like a cup of tea.

"Yes please," Ian replied.

Once Mr Coleman had served the tea along with some delicious looking cakes and scones, he promptly left the room.

An uneasy silence filled the air.

Sir Ian and Father O'Connor had known each other for more than forty years, and neither made a habit of hiding anything from the other, but it suddenly seemed uncomfortable to start a conversation. He suspected that his son was the topic of discussion, but as the priest had invited him over, then he would have to be the one to initiate the conversation.

"Sir Ian," the priest finally stuttered, "I get the feeling that you may have heard already, but recently I was reliably informed by a church member who happens to work in the Crown Prosecution Office that they intend to charge your son with raping a minor and causing grievous bodily harm. To make matters worse, they are also looking at charging him with the rape of his own daughter. Were you aware of this?"

Sir Ian hesitated, then cleared his throat.

"Yes, I heard. As a matter of fact, Donna and I talked about the situation this afternoon. At first, she was hoping that the Kimberleys would agree to settle out of court and the shambolic situation would eventually vanish into thin air, but from what I have been told, Josie Kimberley has insisted that the police hand over the case files to the prosecutors so that Michael can be charged for his crimes. Donna has therefore decided to employ the services of one of the top city defence lawyers."

"But, don't you think that Michael might be convicted and the Doland name tarnished?" the padre asked.

"Father, don't you think that it's a bit too late to care about the family name and reputation? Do you remember before Donna and I left for New Zealand, me telling you about what Michael did to Jennifer's daughter?

Father O'Connor nodded slowly. He remembered.

"Maybe it's time for Donna and me to take responsibility for how we brought the boy up!"

"Ian, I urge you to consider the shame of dragging the Doland name through the mud. Is it worth it? I know how you feel, but I still think you and I should pay the Kimberleys a visit. Maybe, just maybe, we can persuade them to drop the case and change their mind about settling out of court. You know, In hindsight, maybe you and Lady Donna should have stayed down under!"

"Excuse me, Father," Sir Ian interjected. "I may be anything, but I am certainly not a coward. If this is the only way that those two girls, one of which just happens to be my granddaughter, can get justice, then I do not intend to stand in their way."

With that, Sir Ian got up to leave. He patted his friend on the shoulder to reassure him that there were no hard feelings and reiterated his stance about his son's case. He also informed the priest that even his own daughters, Winifred and Jennifer, had threatened to give evidence in court against their only brother.

As he made his way home, the old man once again found himself reminiscing in the back seat of his car. If only he and Donna could have agreed on how to raise Michael, but they just couldn't. Whenever it came to their son's upbringing and discipline, she opposed him all the way. Left to Donna, Michael could do no wrong, and even now, with all the evidence staring her in the face, she was still in denial.

Sir Ian just could not understand what his wife hoped to achieve by hiring a top defence lawyer when even to his jurist mind, the case was an open and shut one.

Sir Ian felt drained, and the last thing he was looking forward to was another argument with his wife. Thankfully, when he got home, she had already left for her beauty class with her cronies. Sir Ian breathed a sigh of relief. He wasn't in the mood for food, so he went straight to his bedroom, washed his hands and face, brushed his teeth, put on his pyjamas and crawled into bed. Soon after he was fast asleep, tossing and turning, dreaming about Michael being handcuffed after losing the case, his wife screaming in court and having a stroke when the jury returned the guilty verdict. Then he saw his son in a prison cell, committing suicide.

He jumped up. The bedsheets were drenched in sweat. It felt so real that Sir Ian was relieved it was only a dream. As much as he blamed his wife for their son's exigencies and delinquent habits, he still loved them both and would do anything to stop what he saw in his dream from coming to pass. Sir Ian tried to go back to sleep, but couldn't. So, he lay awake till dawn.

Meanwhile, Lady Donna returned late and slept in her own bedroom, something she had started doing of late. She also made sure to lock the door as she was in no mood to talk to a man who planned to stand by and watch his only son go to jail.

2
Charles Quinn

Ian was in two minds. "Should he tell Donna about the nightmare or not?"

Considering the current state of their relationship, he wasn't too sure she would want to listen, but he decided he would tell her at breakfast anyway. To his surprise, when he came downstairs for breakfast, the housekeeper told him that his wife had left the house for a so-called urgent appointment.

Sir Ian suspected that she might have gone to see the lawyer and therefore felt it was no longer necessary to tell her about the dream, but there was something about the nightmare that made him feel very uneasy.

Having skipped dinner the day before, Sir Ian was very hungry, but the prospect of eating alone in their huge dining room was not appealing. So, he decided to pour himself a glass of freshly pressed orange juice, sat in the patio and started reading the newspapers. While he was reading and sipping his juice, Sir Ian dozed off. However, what started as a relaxing nap soon turned into another nightmare.

He found himself having a dream similar to the one he had the night before, except this time around, he could see both Donna and Michael accusing him of siding with the enemy. He denied the accusation vehemently, swearing his allegiance and promising to deal with those ingrates, referring to the Kimberleys.

Sir Ian woke up, trembling. "What is happening to me?" he whispered to himself.

As he got up to go back into the house, Lady Donna and Michael walked in totally ignoring his presence. He tried to give his wife a peck on the cheek, but she simply turned and walked out of the room while Michael looked at him with such disdain that Sir Ian began to wonder if his dream had already become a reality.

"Hello Michael," Sir Ian said. "How are you and your family?"

"Father, please do not patronise me," Michael replied in a cold, disrespectful tone. "I know that you have never really cared about me, so there's no need to start trying now."

"What is that supposed to mean?" Sir Ian was taken aback. "I have given you everything a father could ever give a son, but you frittered it all away. Now you're behaving like a spoilt child caught with both hands in the cookie jar. You may have your mother eating out of your hand, but do not think for one second that I do not see through your false façade. Son, you need to wake up and smell the coffee because your mother won't be able to save you this time around."

"Well, at least mum believes in her son, she has always been there for my family and me. I obviously can't say the same about you. In case you haven't realised, if you didn't hate me so much, you wouldn't be blinded to the truth. And by the way, what happened to innocent until proven guilty?"

"What!" Sir Ian could not believe his ears. "Have you taken leave of your senses?"

"Well, with or without you, mum and I intend to take on your innocent Kimberley family, and after we crush them, I will exact my revenge on that lying daughter of..."
"Michael, listen to yourself!" Sir Ian thundered. "Don't you have any moral scruples? You have lied to yourself for so long that you actually believe the lie."

Looking straight into Michael's eyes, the little sympathy he had left for his son seemed to drain away. Inasmuch as he hated to think it, he was gradually beginning to feel that his son was a lost cause. Finally, Sir Ian shook his head and left the room. It was time he had a candid conversation with Michael's mother. Even though he knew it would most likely turn into a massive showdown, he was determined to make sure his wife didn't do something she would end up regretting for the rest of her life.

As Sir Ian walked towards the kitchen, he heard his wife barking instructions at the cook, saying something about expecting special guests that evening. This was news to Sir Ian. When he walked into the kitchen Lady Donna, knowing she had been caught out, lamely told her husband that Mr and Mrs Quinn were coming over for dinner, almost making it sound as if the Quinns had invited themselves over, hence leaving her with no choice.

Sir Ian wasn't exactly chuffed, but right now, he just needed to talk to her.

"Donna, we need to talk," he began.
"Well, I am sure you can see that I am busy at the moment. Can't it wait?"
"No, it can't. I just spoke to Michael, and I must say that I was astounded at the arrogance he exhibited. The boy seems to be under the illusion that the case is as good as won."
"Ian, maybe you need to keep your opinion to yourself. I know you were the head of the Family Division during your

time, but with the new rules and regulations, I would like to hear what Mr Quinn has to say," Lady Donna quipped.

Sir Ian was about to respond harshly when he caught a glimpse of the cook standing by the sink. He stormed out of the kitchen. Neither of them spoke a word to each other until later that evening, after the Quinn's arrival.

Sir Ian knew Charles from his days on the bench as he presided over a number of the lawyer's cases. He remembered how he had to tolerate the man and his insufferable left-wing ideologies at the senior judges and lawyers retreats. Mr Quinn fell into the category of those who wanted to bring down the establishment they railed against, but at the same time enjoy the freedom and perks that went with the job. That was hypocrisy of the highest order, and Sir Ian couldn't stand it. So, he wondered what they were going to talk about, especially as he wasn't the one who invited the couple over for dinner.

By the time Sir Ian finally came downstairs, Lady Donna and Michael were already playing the perfect hosts. They were seated with glasses of wine, and the conversation was flowing. As he walked into the room, the butler asked what he would like to drink, but Sir Ian said he didn't want anything. He greeted Mr and Mrs Quinn before taking his favourite seat. Then he crossed his legs, lit his pipe and fixed his gaze on his wife.

Lady Donna felt a bit uncomfortable, especially as she knew that her husband did not agree with what she was doing, but that was not going to stop her.

"So Ian, like I told you, I have invited Mr Quinn and his wife over for dinner to discuss Michael's upcoming case in court. I felt it would be a good idea for us to discuss the various options available before the hearing."

As Lady Donna rounded up, the butler opened the door to announce that dinner had been served. He held the door open as the Quinns, Lady Donna, Michael and Sir Ian filed into the dining room taking their seats at the table according to the family observance.

Over dinner, everyone seemed to maintain a semblance of civility and decorum, but the more Sir Ian thought about how his wife was trying to hijack a legal process that was best left to the courts, the more he felt anger rise inside him.

After dessert, they retired to the coffee room, and as they sat down, Charles Quinn opened the conversation. He asked Michael directly what had happened between himself and his daughter, Leah, but didn't ask him anything about Josie. Mr Quinn seemed to dismiss Josie's case as a non-issue. It was a mistake he would live ultimately to regret.

3
The Meeting

Michael Doland was arrested and formally charged for the rape of Josie Kimberley and her daughter Leah, and despite Lady Donna's best efforts, he was refused bail based on recommendations from the Crown Prosecution Service.

News of the involvement of some well-known celebrities using young children for sexual gratification, grooming them for paedophilic grooves and passing them from hand to hand, which in some cases led to their outright murder, had consistently been in the media over the past two years. So, when the Press caught a whiff of the Doland boy's arrest, it had them agog. Various reports flooded the media, but none dared make any disparaging remarks about the police investigation and its findings for fear of being labelled "*Paedophile Supporters*".

With a shrinking police force overwhelmed by unproven allegations of what some members of the elite were up to and investigations at an all-time high, the Kimberleys feared their quest for justice could be in danger as the Crown Prosecution Service might jettison their case given the commotion that had accompanied similar accusations.

At the Dolands, things were beginning to fall apart. The lady of the house realised that some of her friends had stopped calling after hearing about Michael's arrest. Her two daughters had also alienated her for making no effort whatsoever to prevent their brother's outrageous behaviour. Left to them, their mother approved of Michael's deeds and saw nothing wrong with her beloved son's character. And as she could no longer rely on her husband, Lady Donna found solace in Mr Quinn's office.

A worried Lady Donna visited Charles Quinn almost every other day. She called him at ungodly hours every night, badgering about the prospects of her son's eventual conviction. However, Mr Quinn continually managed to reassure his client that everything was under control. He confirmed that Michael's wife Elsie was not going to testify against her husband in the matter of little Leah, therefore making it the young girl's word against her father's. He even hinted at having a trump card which he intended to use during the trial; a secret witness that would testify against Josie.

The irony of the whole saga was that previously, Lady Donna being a high society lady and a loyal liberal democrat, could not stand the likes of Mr Quinn because he was a known labour leftist whose views bordered on communism. But now that they shared a common interest, they planned to tear apart the findings of the Police investigation and make it out to be a witch hunt carried out to cash in on the society's horror over the sexual abuse perpetrated on children by the elite.

Both parties, the Kimberleys with the help of their lawyer Mr Salmon Goldberg and the police, and Mr Quinn representing Michael Doland, were determined to slug it out in the courthouse. The hysteria was tangible as news of the upcoming trial was publicised on the front pages of papers and on television networks.

The Police and the Crown Prosecution Service had set up a meeting between the Kimberleys and The Office of the Prosecutor to discuss the modalities of the case, and offer advice on how to handle hostile questioning from the defence, something that was inevitable in rape cases, especially high profile ones like this.

Before their meeting, Angela had asked Mrs Pearce if she wouldn't mind accompanying them. Considering the role Carol had played in bringing Leah's case to the notice of the police, and being Leah's foster mother, Angela knew that her input would come in handy.

As the Kimberleys and Mrs Pearce entered the waiting room reserved for those who had been invited to have their cases reviewed, they were immediately ushered into the senior prosecutor's office. They were surprised to see that she was a woman.

As tea and coffee were served, it dawned on Josie that it was going to be a long session, and she only hoped that she would not get bored once the legal terminology started flying around. Josie never liked courtrooms, and never thought that she would grace one with her presence, but here she was.

The prosecutor cleared her throat.

"I am not sure if you are aware, but the Dolands have employed the services of Charles Quinn QC. When it comes to abuse cases, he is arguably one of the most formidable defence lawyers around. He is responsible for the release of some of the worst sex offenders in the country. My proposal, therefore, will be in line with the rules and regulations recommended in Section 41 of the Youth Justice & Criminal Evidence Act (YJCEA)."

While the prosecutor spoke, Josie tried in vain to figure out what kind of woman she was, but one thing was sure, she knew what she was talking about and was very passionate about it.

"Excuse me Madam Prosecutor," Josie's mother interrupted. "Does it really matter who the defence lawyer is? Both cases seem watertight to me?"
"I understand your concerns Mrs Kimberley, but we cannot assume anything. Allow me to brief you on the provisions of the Evidence Act I just mentioned," the Prosecutor replied.

It was evidently clear that Angela's question had created an uneasiness in the room. Mum was not usually like that, Josie thought.

"You see," the prosecutor continued, "the Act provides that we ask the defence at a pre-trial review if they intend to make an application under this section to admit any of Josie's previous sexual history, which I have come to understand is an issue."

She turned to Josie.

"Josie, I want to assure you that we are here for you and Leah, but we need to cover all the bases. The defence will try to browbeat you with all kinds of assertions of untruths. The question is, "Will you be able to stay strong and not break down?""

The police officer handling the case hadn't said a word until now.

"Madam Prosecutor, Lady Donna has been involved in a high profile campaign to clear her son's name. It goes without saying that she is determined to make sure that the trial is conducted in the public eye."
"Yes, I can assure you that I am aware of what Lady Donna has been up to, but I doubt it will work in her favour. It was agreed from the very beginning, that due to the serious

nature of the crime these cases would be tried by a jury. I must warn you that from opinion polls, the majority of the public tends to blame rape victims, especially if there had been any prior contact with the attacker before the alleged rape. But I believe that justice will prevail, and future victims will once again be encouraged to put their faith in the justice system."

John Kimberley had been listening attentively to the prosecutor, but now as he spoke, one could feel the passion in his voice.

"Many, including members of my own family, have asked why I stopped the police from prosecuting Michael Doland when my daughter accused him of rape. Well, you will find everything and more in this notepad."

John pulled a small notepad out of his blazer pocket and handed it to the prosecutor.

"I have written the exact response I gave to the police at the time, and also what I would do if I were presented with the same situation again. I know I made an unforgivable mistake, but my daughter and my granddaughter do not deserve to suffer the consequences of my appalling judgement. They deserve justice, and I intend to do everything within my power to ensure that they get it."
"Thank you, Mr Kimberley," said the prosecutor. "I must say that in all my years as a barrister I have never come across allegations of this kind. Therefore, anything that will help us win the case is much appreciated. I can assure you that all the circumstances surrounding the case will be looked at in detail. Nothing will be overlooked or taken for granted."

She turned to Josie.

"Young lady, you have nothing to worry about. We have

several witnesses who are more than willing to testify against Michael Doland, and barring any undue interference from the family, Michael's sisters are also willing to appear as prosecution witnesses."

Josie expressed her concern about how the trial might affect Leah, but once again, she was assured that her daughter would not testify in public. The police had already documented Leah's story, and that had been corroborated by what Michael's wife told the police about her husband's weird behaviour towards Leah. They also had medical evidence of genital injuries inflicted on Leah, which were consistent with sexual assault.

The meeting finally came to an end after precisely three hours and twenty-two minutes, and just as Mrs Pearce and the Kimberleys were about to leave the prosecutor's office, she told Josie one last thing.

"Do not be intimidated by the defence counsel. They will try and pressure you into giving specific details about what happened and what you did to try and resist the attack. Going by what you told the police and the school authorities, he slapped and gagged you, and to use the exact words from the Metropolitan Police detective investigator's report, "Any man willing to slap a woman without provocation, would most likely not think twice about raping her - it's just another form of abuse.""

"Thank you," Josie replied, smiling to herself as she walked out of the Senior Prosecutor's Office. Her response brought back memories of Nigeria.

As they made their way to the car park, Josie told her parents that she was going to pick Leah up from school, after which she would drop her off with Mrs Pearce.

"Okay, Josie. See you later then," Angela replied.

Then she turned to Mrs Pearce.

"Carol, thank you so much for coming along. It means so much to me."

"You're welcome, Angela," Carol smiled.

4
Bitter Memories

Josie had been restless since her return from Nigeria. Things were not going the way she thought they should, especially when she realised that there would be a separate hearing for her to obtain leave from the courts if she was to have legal custody of Leah. It seemed unfair and unjustified after everything both of them had already been through. Then, for some reason, it was taking so long for the abuse cases to go to trial. Josie knew the police were doing their best with the Crown Prosecution Service, but she just felt so helpless.

To while away the time, Josie had asked her father if he could get her a part-time job with his company, but she knew that wasn't what she really wanted to do. Over time she had come to realise that there was so much more to life than a nine to five job and had found herself continually toying with the idea of setting up a home for abused children who had nowhere to stay. The more she thought about it and how she could maybe one-day influence lawmakers to be more stringent when deliberating on issues related to the abuse of the vulnerable, the more she felt it was what she had been called to do.

Visiting Leah at Mrs Pearce's house was always an emotional time for Josie, and the last visit was no different. Carol Pearce was a lovely lady; she was pleasant, caring and always treated Leah like one of her own. Josie was given unfettered access to her daughter, all she had to do was inform Mrs Pearce beforehand of her impending visit.

Josie remembered taking in Leah's pretty face and once again blaming herself for running away and leaving the innocent little girl behind. She could never forgive herself for abandoning her daughter, even though the circumstances surrounding her conception were not exactly pleasant. But that wasn't Leah's fault. After all, she was the one who chose not to have an abortion, and that was one decision she would never regret.

Now, as she lay all alone on the couch, she perused what she had been through over the last seven years, how the things she experienced had changed her from a fun-loving, happy-go-lucky girl into a hardcore cynic. Having a Christian upbringing, she knew that wallowing in bitterness and resentment wasn't healthy, but at that very moment, her mind was consumed with getting her revenge on Michael Doland and his evil mother. Strangely, she couldn't remember feeling this way when she was in Nigeria. She could only put it down to seeing Leah, a young, innocent little girl, paying the price for a mistake that was in no way her fault. The thought brought tears to her eyes, and she found herself weeping uncontrollably until she finally fell asleep.

Josie was still fast asleep on the sofa when her mother came back from the supermarket. Angela tried not to disturb her daughter, but the squeaky front door woke her anyway. As Josie sat up, her mother realised that she had been crying.

"What's the matter, Josie?" Angela asked.
"Mum, I don't know what came over me. I guess carrying

the burden of everything that has happened over the years is a lot harder than I thought. I keep trying to erase the memories of the past, but I can't."

"Did something in particular trigger this feeling because, unless I missed something, you've looked pretty fine since you came back from Nigeria?"

"I guess it has to do with my visits to the Pearce's. I always seem to leave her house feeling partly responsible for everything Leah has been through, especially when I remember the dream I had about bringing her up. I'm just finding it really difficult to forgive myself at the moment."

"My dear Josie, you need to stop torturing yourself. None of us, especially your dad and I, have handled this situation properly. My prayer is that hopefully one day we can all make amends."

"It's not just that, mum. My heart breaks each time I see her. To be conceived by rape, raped by a rapist father and go through all that pain with hardly any support; it's just too much. How can I forgive myself for letting all that happen to her?"

Seeing the pain on her daughter's face, Angela leaned in and gave Josie a big, warm hug.

Finally, Josie wiped away her tears.

"Mum, do you know if a date has been set for the trial yet? Since the Magistrate court appearance and subsequent transfers to the Crown Court, everything seems to have ground to a halt."

"Be patient, my dear. Your father is in discussions with the police; he's handling that side of things. I'm sure we will be informed as soon as the date is set. For now, I suggest you concentrate on building your relationship with Leah because it will help settle things with Social Services in the near future."

With that, Angela stood up, picked up the shopping bags, and went to the kitchen.

Josie knew her mother was right. She had to stop brooding and stay focused on the matter at hand. At least she had the comfort of knowing that there was no statute of limitation on rape cases.

While in Nigeria, she had made herself a promise to publish her memoir when she got back to England. She planned to include everything; her sickening ordeal with Michael, her choice to give birth to little Leah, the trip to Scotland, meeting her long lost friend Bosede, staying with the Archibongs in Lagos, and every other thing that had happened in between. She also wanted to find out from Mrs Pearce what actually transpired when she found Leah at the railway station.

"I might as well start working on my journal," Josie thought to herself.

She was determined to put it all down not just for herself, but also for the benefit of other vulnerable young girls so that they would not make the same mistakes she made.

Josie found herself replaying her ordeal with Michael in her head, over and over again, trying to identify where she slipped up. Had she encouraged him in any way, or given him the impression that she wanted more than a teacher-pupil relationship? The only mistake Josie could place her finger on was the time she spent alone with Michael in the classroom going through the Bible. All she was sincerely trying to do was help him find a solution to the negative reputation he had built within and outside the school walls. Only God knows what was going through his dirty, depraved mind. Teachers were supposed to protect their pupils, not take advantage of them. She was an impressionable, young teenager, and he had no right whatsoever to take undue advantage of her.

Josie had heard about how, out of fear, some rape victims chose not to appear in court, but she was more than ready to confront Michael and give evidence against him. Though she did not know what Michael's defence planned to throw at her, Josie had steeled herself for the trial; she was not going to be intimidated, nor was she going to back down. Michael had to pay for what he did, and even if she didn't receive justice for herself, she was sure that little Leah's case would nail the brute to the wall.

Jumping off the sofa, a determined look in her eyes, Josie told herself that there was no room for depression. There was way too much at stake.

5
Grandma Bertha

As soon as it became public knowledge that their father had been arrested, Michael Doland's children, Michael Jr, Dora May and Frances were pulled out of their boarding school.

Their mother Elsie, with the help of her parents, had decided that under the circumstances it would be better to move the children to a school nearer home to avoid them being bullied by fellow pupils who knew about their father's predicament. But not too long after, things started going wrong. Michael Jr hated the new school, and he gradually became a rebel and a recluse openly disobeying his mother at every turn.

On the other hand, because their mother had taken to late nights and alcohol, Dora May more often than not found herself taking care of the house and protecting her little sister Frances from Michael Jr, who was no longer the fun-loving big brother they used to know. She tried to reach out to him, often knocking on his bedroom door, which was now permanently locked, so they could talk, but it was in vain; Michael Jr always shouted at her and told her to mind her own business. It was fair to say that life had become a nightmare.

One night when their mother was out on one of her usual jaunts, little Frances tripped and fell down the stairs. While Dora May tried to comfort her little sister, who was crying in pain, she screamed for help. Michael Jr heard the commotion and immediately opened his door. On seeing what had happened, he promptly picked up the phone and called for an ambulance as he ran down the stairs. Exaggerating his story to grab their attention, he told the person on the other end of the phone that his sister was dying and that they should please hurry.

Tearfully he hugged Dora May asking her to forgive him for his selfishness.

"I forgive you, Michael, but now more than ever we need to stick together," Dora May cried.
"I know Dora, and I'm sorry."

While they waited for the ambulance, Michael Jr called their grandmother, Elsie's mum and told her what had happened to Frances.

"Alright my dear, but where is your mother? Isn't she there?" Bertha asked, trying not to panic.
"She is not here, grandma. She's hardly ever here nowadays."
"Alright, stay calm. I am on my way."

Grandma Bertha arrived a few minutes after the paramedics and made straight for where her granddaughter was being treated. While one of the paramedics asked the older children for details about what happened, the other checked Frances' vitals. Then they carefully strapped the little girl to a stretcher and carried her into the ambulance.

As they rushed her to the hospital, Dora May held Frances' hand

and gently stroked her hair.

"You are going to be fine, little one," Dora May whispered into her ear.

Bertha turned to look at her grandson while they drove behind the ambulance. Even though she knew the boy was still in shock, she sensed there was something deeper. Something wasn't right.

"Have you and your sisters had dinner yet?" she asked as they pulled into the hospital car park.
"Dora was warming something for us to eat when the accident happened," Michael Jr replied.
"Well, I think the hospital cafeteria is open twenty-four hours a day. So hopefully, once we know what condition Frances is in, we can get something to eat."
"Thank you, grandma Bertha."

As they walked into the waiting area, they saw Dora May sitting down with her head in her hands. Michael sat down beside her and placed a comforting arm around his sister's shoulders.

"It is going to be alright. Frances will be fine."
"I hope so because if she isn't, I don't think I will ever forgive myself."
"It is more my fault than yours. I have behaved like a total jerk since this saga with dad kicked off. I should have been there for both of you, but instead, I was only thinking about myself. I'm so sorry, Dora."

Bertha wondered where her daughter was. Why did she leave the children at home all alone, and why had Michael Jr called her instead of his mother?

While they waited for a doctor to brief them on Frances' condition,

Dora May fell asleep and had a dream. She dreamt their mother had died in an accident, their father had been given a life sentence and to make matters even worse, she and her siblings were transferred to different foster homes. She saw people mocking them, calling them all sorts of ugly names and her brother had become a gang member. Dora May woke up frightened, shivering and crying simultaneously.

"Hey, my little one, what is the matter?" Bertha asked, cuddling her granddaughter to her bosom.

At that moment, the consultant who just happened to be the family doctor walked into the waiting room smiling. From the x-ray, Frances had sustained multiple fractures to her right arm and left leg but being young, she should heal well over time. Then, the doctor suddenly looked around as if he remembered something.

"Michael, where is your mum? Why isn't she here?" He asked.

Bertha quickly jumped in, lying to protect her daughter.

"My daughter went out for the night and asked me to help look after the children. I was in the kitchen, making dinner when I heard Frances scream. It is all my fault; I shouldn't have taken my eyes off them."

If the doctor doubted Bertha's words, he did not show it. He told them that Frances had been admitted to the children's ward and that they should be able to see her soon. Then he ushered them into his office and offered them something to eat.

While Dora May and Michael Jr gobbled down the sandwiches, burgers and chips, and Bertha sipped her tea, the doctor told them how he wasn't actually supposed to be on duty that night. However, because his colleague who went for a conference in Scotland had

had his flight cancelled due to dense fog, he was called in to cover.

Not too long after the refreshments, they were told they could see Frances, but when they got to her room, the little girl was sound asleep with her leg and arm in a cast.

"Grandma, is it okay if we stay with Frances?" Michael Jr asked.
"We would really like to be here when she wakes up," Dora May said, her eyes pleading with the old woman.
"Not to worry children, we are all going to be here when Frances wakes up," Bertha smiled.
"Thank you, grandma," Dora May and Michael Jr echoed.

Before too long, the children were asleep, and though she was feeling exhausted, there was way too much on Bertha's mind. As she watched her three grandchildren, she wondered what they had been going through, especially as their mother seemed to have abandoned them to fend for themselves. The more she thought about her daughter's irresponsible behaviour, the angrier she became. But at the same time, it dawned on her that maybe she was partly to blame.

Even though Elsie never told her what Michael Doland was up to, there were several occasions when Bertha wanted to ask but didn't because she was afraid to hear what her daughter's response would be. Now the consequences of her son in law's escapade had caught up with the rest of his family, and unfortunately, the only way his wife knew how to handle the situation was by throwing all caution to the wind, partying all night and getting drunk.

Thoughts of how she had objected to her daughter marrying the Doland boy came flooding back. Everyone, including her husband, thought he was a charming, respectful young man, but

Bertha wasn't deceived. She knew a selfish, inconsiderate man when she saw one. However, Elsie insisted on marrying Michael, and with the full support of her father, who was more interested in his daughter taking on the Doland name, her hands were tied. When they eventually tied the knot and started having children, she remembered praying and hoping that Michael would prove her wrong. Unfortunately, he didn't.

Now, all she could do was protect her grandchildren, and make sure that no harm came to them as a result of their parents' thoughtless, selfish behaviour. And if it so happened that her daughter was deemed incapable of looking after the children, then she was determined to be there for them no matter what. Her grandchildren would lack nothing.

Bertha was still deep in thought when the nurse came into the room. Initially, she was taken aback as this was not the same nurse who had tended to Frances earlier on, but when she caught a glimpse of sunlight through the blinds, Bertha realised that time had flown by, and this nurse must have just started her shift.

As the nurse walked towards the patient's bed, Dora May and Michael Jr woke up. So did little Frances.

"Where is mummy? I want my mummy," Frances screamed.

Bertha jumped up and placed a comforting arm around her teary-eyed little granddaughter.

"It's alright, Frances. Mummy is on her way, but you have to let the nurse help if you want to get better."
"Okay grandma," Frances whispered in between sniffles.

6
Elsie

As Bertha pulled up in front of her daughter's house, Dora May and Michael Jr noticed that the garage door was still wide open and their mother's car was not there. Suddenly Dora May remembered her dream. She leapt out of the car, opened the front door, darted into the house, raced upstairs. Lo and behold, there was her mother snoring away, still wearing the clothes she wore the night before. Dora May stood there staring at her with utter loathing.

Not too long after, she heard grandma Bertha and her brother walking hastily up the stairs. They both stood behind Dora May and watched with dismay as Elsie slept without a care in the world, completely oblivious of what happened the night before.

After being glued silently to one spot for what seemed like an age, Dora May and Michael Jr went to their rooms to freshen up leaving their grandmother standing in the doorway. After a while, Bertha hissed and shook her head before making her way to the kitchen to fix breakfast for the kids.

While they were sitting at the dining table, eating breakfast, they heard the stairs creak. Elsie slowly made her way down the steps, and as she walked into the kitchen to make herself a cup of coffee to help with her terrible hangover, she was shocked to see three pairs of eyes staring back at her as if she was a ghost.

"What was her mother doing here," Elsie thought.

Finally, without saying a word, Elsie pulled out a chair, sat at the table and poured herself a cup of coffee, which had just been brewed by her mother. After the look of resentment and bitterness she had seen on her children's faces, and the anger and disappointment on her mother's, Elsie made a conscious effort to look away as she sipped her coffee. Bertha could take no more.

"Elsie," she began, "where were you last night? Why did you leave these children at home all alone?"
"Mum, please don't start. Before I left the house yesterday evening, I gave the housekeeper strict instructions on what she had to do before leaving for the weekend. I came back as soon as I could and did not want to wake the children."
"You are a liar!" her mother yelled. "How dare you lie so brazenly about coming home as soon as you could. Do you not have any shame?"
"Mum if you say you came back as soon as you could and didn't want to disturb us, why is your car not in the garage?" Michael Jr asked with an inquisitive tone. "Even now you reek of alcohol and cigarettes. What is the matter with you?"
"Don't you dare talk to me like that young man. It's not my fault that your useless father got arrested?"
"Mum, haven't you realised that Frances isn't here?" Dora May asked, almost in tears. "If not for grandma, we would still be at the hospital, or maybe with Social Services in a foster home."
"No need to exaggerate young lady," Elsie replied sarcastically. "Where is Frances anyway, and what is all that nonsense about being in the hospital?"

"Shame on you, Elsie," Bertha shouted, giving her daughter a frosty look. "I know I did not bring you up like this. Look at the beautiful children God has blessed you with, yet you want to throw that away because you're struggling to handle a simple trial? Well, if you really want to know, Frances has been admitted to the hospital with multiple fractures to her arm and leg. And you better thank God because, from what I gathered, it could have been a lot worse."

"Oh no," Elsie screamed in panic. "I am so sorry."

It was while they were all seated at the table and going over what happened the night before that a hippie-looking young man parked Elsie's car in front of the garage. Then, to Bertha's amazement, he invited himself into the house. With bleary eyes and reeking of alcohol and tobacco smoke, he rudely asked someone to get him something to eat. Bertha could take no more. The old lady jumped up and told him that, if he did not leave at once, she would call the police. Startled, the young man immediately began to back out of the house throwing Elsie a wink as he told her to meet him at the usual place, at the same time.

"My daughter is in hospital, so I won't be able to see you tonight, but I will call you," Elsie giggled unashamedly.

"Elsie, I would advise you to go upstairs right now before I do something that we will both regret," her mother said in a cold, stern tone.

Elsie knew that voice. Her mother only used it when she was about to flip. Elsie remembered how her mum always seemed to appear docile despite her husband's high handedness and arrogance. But whenever she was pushed to the wall, she showed a side of her that both Elsie and her dad feared.

Without saying another word, Elsie pushed her chair back, stood up and stomped up the staircase like a spoilt child.

Standing under the shower, she remembered the numerous times when little Leah would come running to her for a hug or any sign of affection, but she just could not bring herself to love the girl. She resented her. She remembered the children's last exeat before they were pulled out of school. Michael Jr, Dora May and Frances came home to find that Leah had gone. When they asked her where their sister was, she rebuffed them and refused to answer.

Elsie was shocked when one day, her son came home holding an old newspaper. While she and her husband were watching TV, Michael Jr stood right in front of them, lifted the paper and pointed to a picture of Leah. Then he shouted to Dora May to come downstairs. Dora ran down and was a bit surprised at the scene before her. Michael Jr then read out what Leah had told the reporter about not having any parents, her grandparents living in faraway New Zealand and what the man she called father had done to her.

Michael Jr demanded to know what was going on, and even though they had tried to lie about Leah's accusation, Elsie knew that the children did not buy it. The words her daughter spoke still haunted her till that very day.

"Mum, Dad, if it is true, your sins will find you out!"

Recently with everything that was going on, the thought had crossed her mind that maybe they were paying for what Michael did to the little girl. However, she could not bring herself to admit that she played a part in the abuse of the poor child. Elsie convinced herself that, since Leah was foisted on her by Michael and his meddlesome mother, then it simply wasn't her fault.

Since Elsie had refused to tell the children the truth, Bertha took it upon herself to explain to Michael Jr and Dora May what was said to have happened between their father, Josie and little Leah. She felt it was the only way to prepare them for the pain, shame and public humiliation they would most surely face once everyone caught wind of the situation. That didn't go down well with Elsie.

"What right did the old woman have to interfere and poison the minds of my children against their father?" Elsie could feel resentment building up inside her.

As the warm water gently massaged her body, Elsie suddenly shuddered. There she was engrossed in her own selfish thoughts while her little daughter was lying on a hospital bed. What was the matter with her? It was as if her life was slipping away right before her very eyes. As tears rolled down her wet face, Elsie decided that if for nothing else, for the sake of the children, she had to make an effort to turn her life around.

She knew it was not going to be easy. She had hidden bottles of vodka and packs of cigarettes in every corner of the house. Her body constantly craved the flow of alcohol and the buzz of nicotine. It was as if her life depended on it. It was so bad that she was rapidly losing weight because she no longer bothered to eat proper food. Elsie attributed her weight loss to the travail she and her family were going through, but she knew that was a lie.

Her mother had confronted her about her alcohol abuse, and her friends advised her to take it easy on the booze, linking it to the paleness of her skin and the loss of her natural beauty. But Elsie was living in denial. She simply cut off anyone who questioned her irrational behaviour. The truth was it was the only way she knew how to deal with the shame of her husband's child abuse saga.

Elsie had not visited her husband since his arrest, and she had no plans to, not after everything he had put her through. Her evil mother-in-law had called her several times, leaving messages reminding her of her responsibility to stand by her husband. Elsie despised Lady Donna, especially as she believed it was the old woman's meddling and selfishness that got Michael into this mess in the first place.

As she stepped out of the shower, she wanted to lash out. Nobody, including her family, understood what she was going through and instead of sympathising with her, all they did was judge and condemn her. She was done listening to everyone. She knew she wasn't thinking rationally, but she didn't care.

Elsie slipped into a pair of dark blue jeans, a white t-shirt and a cardigan, slapped on some makeup and was just about to go downstairs to ask if anyone wanted to follow her to the hospital when her mother, without knocking, opened the door.

"And where do you think you're going looking like that?" she asked.
"Where else would I be going to, mum? I am obviously off to the hospital to see my daughter. You are welcome to come with me if you wish," Elsie replied sarcastically.
"Don't you think your lipstick is too bright? You are going to see an injured child, not one of your boyfriends."
"Mother, it is none of your business," Elsie snapped. "All my life, I have been told what to and what not to do. Not anymore! From now on, I live my life the way I want to, so please back off. I will let you know if I need your advice."

Elsie did not know that her children were by the door listening until she saw them. They heard everything their mother said. For a split second, Elsie's head dropped. Then putting on a brave face, she picked up her handbag, pushed past her mother and walked through the door announcing that she was off to the hospital as she made her way down the stairs.

Michael Jr and Dora May were gobsmacked. They watched as their mother strutted through the front door before slowly making their way to the kitchen to tidy up. They both came to the conclusion that they could no longer rely on their mother, and for the foreseeable future, they were going to have to depend on their grandmother for guidance.

"Children, what are your plans for today?" grandma Bertha asked.
"Well, we were hoping that you could take us to the hospital later this afternoon, and then go to your place afterwards if it's okay with you?"
"Of course," she replied, trying to hide her surprise.

From what Frances had told her when she visited that morning, it was obvious that the lines under her mother's eyes were the result of a sleepless night, and after what she said earlier that morning, Elsie knew she owed her mother an apology. She had also sensed for a while that her children were slowly slipping away from her. Elsie knew it was all her fault, and as much as she wanted to make amends, the only thing her body seemed to crave nowadays was a drink. If she was to win back the children's trust, she was going to have to find a way to resist the temptation for alcohol.

"One day at a time, Elsie, one day at a time," she whispered to herself.

To set the ball rolling, Elsie decided that once she got back home, she would make lunch for everyone, and then they would all visit Frances as a family.

While she was in the kitchen preparing her surprise, family-bonding lunch, Dora May walked in.

"Mum, Michael and I are about to leave for the hospital with grandma. From there, we plan to go back to hers. We were thinking of sleeping over if you don't mind?"

"But sweetheart, I was hoping we could all sit down and have lunch, then go and visit Frances together. What do you say to that hmm?"

"Well, you might have to speak to grandma about that."

"What!" Elsie shrieked angrily.

"Mum, I don't want to argue with you. I only asked you to speak to grandma. Please," Dora May said in a controlled, soft-toned voice.

Elsie stormed out of the kitchen to confront her mother, who was resting on the couch in the living room.

"Mum, my daughter just informed me that she and her brother are planning on sleeping over at yours tonight. Is this true?"

"My dear, when you went to visit Frances, I asked Dora May and her brother what they wanted to do today, and they said they would like to spend the night at mine. I hope that is okay? I would have told you anyway, and if you are up for it, you could come over too. You know that you are always welcome," Bertha smiled.

"Mother, why are you undermining my authority? The children already resent me, especially after what happened last night. I am trying to be a good mother and all you are doing is complicating issues."

The old lady was surprised at her daughter's tone, but she was in no mood to argue. She picked up her handbag and told the children that she would see them at the hospital later on in the day as she hurried towards the front door. Dora May ran after her grandmother and apologised for the misunderstanding. She blamed herself for what had just transpired between the two women.

"My dear child, it is not your fault."

The old lady assured her granddaughter that she was not offended, but that it would be better for her to leave before the situation blew up into an unnecessary ugly scene. She bade her granddaughter goodbye and entered her car.

Dora May stood on the driveway and watched until her grandma's car disappeared into the distance before going indoors to talk to her brother. She found him going through some papers in their father's study.

"What are you doing, Michael?" she asked.

"I am looking for Leah's adoption papers. I still remember the night they brought Leah to the house. Even though I heard mum and dad arguing I didn't understand why until the rape story surfaced. Dora, do you think dad did all the things he is being accused of, and if he did why didn't mum do something?"

"I don't know, Michael, but what I do know is that Leah is and will always be our little sister. I do not care how she was conceived. I have always loved her, and I know Frances still misses her even though she does not talk about it."

"Alright, but we cannot let mum know about what we plan to do," Michael cautioned as he closed the file that held the adoption documents. He couldn't help but notice a letter confirming that the Kimberleys did not relinquish their visitation rights, reserving the right to visit Leah from time to time.

Michael Jr and Dora May both agreed that they would wait for the right time before making their move.

7
Finding Leah

Two days after Frances was admitted to hospital, her older siblings decided it was time to start their search for Leah. They had successfully wormed out some information about the Kimberleys from their grandmother, who though suspicious, was unaware of what her two grandchildren were up to.

Dora May and Michael Jr did not know where Leah was staying, but they assumed that the Kimberleys would know. So, on that May Bank holiday Monday, they persuaded their father's driver to take them to the Kimberleys residence.

The sound of the doorbell surprised the Kimberleys. They were not expecting visitors and could really do with a peaceful lie in. However, as the person ringing the bell persisted, John decided to find out who was there. When he opened the door, he saw a boy clutching a bouquet of flowers and a girl holding what looked like a gift bag.

"Hello, Sir," both of them chorused.
"Hello. How can I help you?" Mr Kimberley asked, looking

slightly confused.

Angela was also curious to know who was at the door and when she got there, she was as surprised as her husband. "Who were these children?" she thought.

After a brief silence, Michael Jr finally mustered up some courage.

"My name is Michael, and this is my sister Dora May, "he stuttered. "We have come to see Leah, our sister. We were told that she stays here."

"Sir, please can we see her," Dora May pleaded.

It suddenly dawned on John and Angela that they had come face to face with Michael Doland's children. Angela invited them into the sitting room and offered them something to drink, but they both shook their heads adamantly. All they wanted was to see Leah.

"So, how did you get here?" John asked.

"Our dad's driver brought us. He is waiting outside. We have heard a few unpleasant things, but we don't care. Leah is our sister, and we love her, and there is nothing anyone can do to change that."

"Alright, my dear," Mrs Kimberley replied, looking at Dora May. "Unfortunately, Leah is not here. Since the incident with the police, and her admission to the hospital, she has been taken into foster care and currently lives with the kind lady who found her at the train station."

"Does your mother know that you are here?" John asked, an air of suspicion in his voice.

"No sir, she doesn't. The truth is no one knows. Michael and I decided to come on our own. We tricked our grandmother into giving us your address after she told us about your daughter. We are so sorry for everything she went through."

"There is no need for you to be sorry for what your father did. He is an adult, and he will soon face the consequences of his actions," said Mr Kimberley.

After some more awkward silence, Michael Jr turned to Mrs Kimberley.

"Can you please tell us where Leah is?" Michael whispered.
"I wish I could, but due to the pending court case, I can't. However, our daughter visits Leah regularly. In fact, I believe she went to see her today. So, all I can do is ask Josie to tell Leah that you both came looking for her," Angela replied.
"Can we at least leave these flowers and the gift for her?" Michael Jr asked. "Maybe the next time your daughter visits Leah, she could take them along?"
"Are you sure you want to do that?" Angela asked.
"Yes, we are," they both said.

As John and Angela walked the children to the front door, Dora May turned to them with tears in her eyes.

"We may be young, but we are not dumb. What dad did was appalling, and there is no excuse for why mum did not protect Leah. But if you can, please forgive my parents."

Touched by the care, maturity, and wisdom shown by the two children, John and Angela hugged both of them and made it clear that they had no hard feelings towards them and hoped to see them again once things had settled down.

Michael Jr respectfully asked the Kimberleys not to follow them to the car as they did not want the driver to know who they had come to visit. So, respecting their wish, the couple opened the door and waved the children goodbye.

They both breathed a sigh of relief as they sat in the car, amazed that they had actually managed to pull it off. Michael Jr turned to Dora May.

"Do you think they will tell Leah that we came to see her?"
"I think so. They seem like a nice couple, so I guess we can
trust them."
"I'm not too sure about that, Dora. We happen to be the
children of the monster who raped both their daughter and
granddaughter. If I were in their shoes, I know what I would
do."
"Keep your voice down, Michael," Dora May said sternly,
reminding her brother that they were not alone as she
noticed how the driver seemed to slightly turn his head as if
to listen in on what they were saying.
"Okay, but there is no need to take that tone with me. I am
your big brother remember," Michael Jr whispered angrily.
"Then act like one!" Dora May replied, before turning to
look out of the window.

The ride home was a quiet one as both siblings, though in their
own little world, were surprisingly thinking about the same thing.
Thoughts of the seemingly insignificant things that their father
did, like when he told Frances to move out of the room she shared
with Leah, asking her to sleep in the same room as Dora May. Poor
little Frances had told her big sister that she often heard someone
come into the room while both she and Leah were sleeping, but
Dora May put it down to her little sister's overactive imagination.
Now, it dawned on them that it must have been their father all
along.

Michael Jr resented his father for everything he had put their
family through and hearing that their grandmother was planning
on using her influence to bail their father out made the young
boy's blood boil.

"How deceitfully convenient! How can a person rape anyone,

let alone their own child? Gruesome! I hope he never sets foot inside this house again," Michael Jr whispered under his breath.

By the time they drove into the driveway, Dora May and Michael Jr were both sober and in no mood to talk to anyone, especially their mum.

However, when they walked into the house, they saw their mother sprawled on the couch with an empty glass in her hand, her speech incoherent. There were two bottles of vodka on the table; one was empty and the other half full. Dora May quietly walked up to her mum and gently slipped the glass out of her fingers. Then she poured the remaining vodka down the kitchen sink.

"Mother, what has come over you?" Michael Jr thundered, looking at his mum with venom in his eyes.

Dora May, fearing the worst, quickly stepped in, but it soon became apparent that their mother was plastered, so what they said or did was of little significance.

The siblings were still thinking of what to do when they heard the sound of a car pulling up in front of the house. They were relieved to see that it was grandma Bertha with bags of shopping. That was when it dawned on them that they hadn't even had breakfast. They suddenly felt very hungry. Dora May and Michael Jr left their mother in her state of stupor and rushed to hug their grandma, almost pushing the old woman over in the process.

"Wow, what's with all the hugs and kisses?" Then she noticed Dora May's red eyes. "What's wrong, you both look sad?"
"We are just happy to see you, grandma," Dora May replied, trying to cover up what the old lady would soon see once she entered the house.

The three of them walked into the kitchen, Elsie's mum shaking her head as she noticed her daughter splayed across the couch. They had finished unpacking the bags and were about to make something to eat when they heard a big bang in the sitting room. Dora May and Michael Jr, with grandma Bertha following close behind, rushed to the sitting room to find Elsie brandishing her husband's hunting gun. They were all relieved to see that she had not shot herself. Instead, she had shot at one of the wedding pictures hanging on the wall. Michael Jr walked slowly towards his mother, prised out the gun from her hands before pushing her to the ground, and calling her a useless mother.

"Don't you ever talk to your mother like that, young man. No matter what she may have done, she is still your mother, and you must always respect her," grandma Bertha rebuked Michael Jr.
"But gran, didn't you see the empty bottles of vodka in the kitchen, and the drunken state she is in? Is that the mother you want me to respect?"

The old lady did not respond immediately, but instead took a long look at her daughter. Then with a tired sounding voice spoke to her.

"Elsie, even if your back is against the wall, that is no excuse for this kind of behaviour. I hope you know that the Dolands will look for any excuse to take the children away from you, so you need to get your act together and do so quickly. Go upstairs, sort yourself out, and come and get something to eat."

For the children, the old lady's words created a sense of deja vu; the second time in the space of two days that their grandma had told their mum to get her act together.

Elsie eventually managed to stand up and stared at the blurred images of her mum and children before staggering up the stairs, holding on to the railings as if her life depended on it. Then as she stumbled through the door to her room, she fell to the floor and passed out. They waited patiently for Elsie to come back downstairs, and when after about an hour, there was no sign of her, Dora May decided to check.

Dora screamed! There on the floor, in a pool of blood, was her mother.

The paramedic's arrived within fifteen minutes, and after stabilising her, they placed Elsie on a bed, rolled her into the ambulance, and drove to the hospital. Once again, for Dora May and Michael Jr, there was a sense of déjà vu, the second time in two days that they had witnessed a member of the family being ferried away in an ambulance.

Just like the last time, grandma Bertha and the children drove behind the ambulance to the same hospital where their sister Frances was staying. Bertha had a worried look in her eyes. Elsie was her only child, and the last thing she wanted was to lose her daughter. At that point, she was ready to forgive and forget everything her daughter had done if it would only save her life.

The doctor who attended to Elsie on her arrival to the Accident & Emergency ward had assured them that even though the blood loss was substantial, she was going to be okay. The doctor informed Elsie's mother that they had inserted an intravenous drip as it seemed like her daughter had not eaten properly in the last forty-eight hours. Another worrying observation was Elsie's high blood alcohol level, and even though they had managed to stabilise her, they planned to keep her overnight for precautionary reasons.

While they were there, Dora May and Michael Jr seized the opportunity to see Frances and were pleased when they were told that their little sister would be discharged the following day.

"Finally, some good news," Dora May thought to herself.

8

Injustice

When Josie came back from the Pearce's, her parents told her about the courtesy call they had received from the Doland children.

"The visit took your dad and me by surprise, but they came across as lovely, well-behaved children. What was touching was that they were so apologetic for what their parents had done, and it was hard not to feel sorry for them. It is just unfortunate that their father was such a monster."

Josie did not quite know what to make of the Doland children's visit, and her mother handing her the gifts they brought did not make things any easier. For some reason, the card sticking out of the gift bag caught Josie's attention. She picked it out, opened it and began to read the wobbly looking handwriting. The children described how they missed Leah so much, expressed their heartfelt love for her and wished that she would come home soon. Then in the bottom right corner of the card, they surreptitiously penned a telephone number.

Visibly touched by what the children had written, Josie took a minute to weigh the consequences of calling the number on the card. Her daughter often spoke fondly of the Doland children, she clearly missed them too, and why should the children suffer so much pain because of the sins of their parents. Eventually, Josie came to the conclusion that talking to them might not be as bad an idea as she initially thought.

While her parents waited for her to say something, Josie smiled and slowly walked up the stairs to her room, taking the flowers and the gift bag with her. John and Angela were not sure what to make of their daughter's reaction, but they did not have to wait too long to find out.

Josie's parents were still anxiously sitting on the living room couch when their daughter came downstairs, clutching a large, brown envelope. They stared at her nervously as she sat down beside them. Josie opened the envelope and started going through the contents. When she finally looked up, they could see a sadness in her eyes. Angela and John immediately assumed that something must have gone terribly wrong during her visit to Leah.

"Mum, Dad, do you remember my friend in Lagos, Bosede?

Josie's parents nodded slowly trying to make sense of what was going on.

"She sent me this."

Josie handed the papers to her parents. The more they looked at the paper clippings, the further their heads dropped. Josie began to quote the headings, her voice shaking.

"'Royal Marine 34, rapes and strangles young woman', 'British tourist 28, raped and murdered near Goa beach during Holi festival celebrations', 'Policeman, 48 who thought he was God's gift to womankind jailed for five years after being found guilty of multiple rape counts', 'Paedophile footballer who was found guilty of raping 'besotted' fan, given short sentence after losing appeal', 'Fifteen-year-old girl claims that father regularly pays her for sex', 'Man 33, cleared of raping 22-year-old student after victim commits suicide midway through police investigation',…"

John slowly lowered the paper in his hand.

"Josie, why are you tormenting yourself."

"Dad, is that what you think this is?" Josie tried to stay calm. "I am not tormenting myself, I just want you to see what the world has become; a place that no longer protects the victim. I really don't care what you think, but I am not going to sit back and watch others go through the same ugly experience that I went through. I intend to do something about it!"

"But Josie, don't you think you are a bit too young to get involved in all this?" The concern was evident in her mother's voice.

"Please, can I continue?" Josie asked, trying her best not to lose her patience with her parents. Without giving them another chance to butt in, she continued. "'British backpacker gang-raped and murdered in Goa', 'I thought I would be raped and shot in the head', tearful young woman relives the horrific night she was held at gunpoint by robbers in her apartment', 'I am relieved that he is dead!', says the doctor who discovered that her paedophile husband had abused their four-year-old daughter before taking his life', 'Brave woman abused by Rotherham sex gang ringleader as a teenager reveals how she was groomed by the controlling paedophile and became pregnant at the age of fifteen', 'Man who raped six-year-old girl more than two hundred times while high on drugs and alcohol, jailed for sixteen years.'"

Finally, Josie stopped.

"All I am trying to highlight here is that we always hear about one reform or the other, and how alleged rape victims will no longer face live cross-examination in court, but it's all one big lie! The courts in this country are way too lenient when it comes to sentencing perpetrators of sexual violence. That is why I prefer the American system; once the accused is found guilty, they often receive a real-life sentence, sometimes without parole.

From the research I have done, alleged rape victims will now be able to give evidence via a pre-recorded video that will be played to the jury, and apparently, cross-examinations will also be pre-recorded for all adult sex offences. According to the Justice Secretary, "this will allow judges to cut out the inappropriate cross-examination of rape victims,", but personally I think it is too little too late. Every victim deserves justice, period!"

"Alright Josie we can see your point of view, but you do know that some abusers have been abused themselves, hence…"

"Dad, what are you saying?" He was beginning to get on her nerves. "To even contemplate such discourse is accepting and upholding their evil behaviour as acceptable."

"But Josie, you didn't let me finish. Have you considered the fact that some so-called rape victims actually make up allegations against innocent people who themselves are trashed in court, their lives forever ruined because of a mistaken prosecution?"

"Dad, those cases are few and far between, and you know it!"

"My dear, your father is only playing devil's advocate here," Angela tried to douse the tension.

She knew her husband was only trying to make their daughter see that not all men were monsters, but the last thing they needed right now was a heated argument.

Having successfully calmed the tension in the room, Angela smiled, got up, and invited both her husband and daughter to join her in the kitchen for a hot cup of tea. They both obliged, but Josie was determined to make her thoughts known and no one, not even her parents were going to shut her up.

9
Lilly Ann

Preoccupied with her plans to fight for justice for rape victims, Josie had all but forgotten about Lilly Ann's wedding, which was just around the corner.

Lilly Ann had asked Josie to be her chief bridesmaid, and even though both families had assumed that she would be happy to play the role, Josie declined. Instead, she opted to be one of the bridesmaids. Somehow, after her brother told her that one of his friends was going to be the best man, Josie managed to convince herself that the reason why Lilly Ann chose her was to matchmake her with Bruce's friend, which was the last thing she wanted.

Josie suddenly remembered that the bridesmaids had a fitting appointment with the dressmaker the following day. Personally, she would have preferred for the court hearing to be over and done with so that she could be totally focussed on Lilly Ann's wedding, but unfortunately, that was not the case, and as much as Josie tried to put her pending court appearance out of her mind she was constantly reminded of it, thanks to the media. In moments like these, she wished she was back in Lagos living her life without a care in the world.

She had planned to meet up with Lilly Ann for a coffee at an Italian café along Kensington High Street, and since she was not sure when she would be back, Josie told her mum that she might be a bit late. Josie grabbed her scarf and handbag and surprisingly felt at peace as she walked to the bus stop breathing in the fresh air. It was a feeling Josie hadn't felt for quite some time. She needed to clear the negative thoughts that were swimming around in her mind, and the walk seemed to do the trick. In fact, she enjoyed her little walk so much that she decided to get off the bus three stops before the café to do some window shopping.

While she was looking through a shop window, she felt a tap on her shoulder. It was Akin, Bosede's cousin! Josie couldn't believe her eyes. They had often met at parties, weddings and family gatherings when she was in Nigeria, and even though they had totally opposite personalities, they surprisingly got along well.

"Hello Josie, you look like you just saw a ghost. You do remember me?"
"Of course, I remember you. It's just that you were the last person I expected to see," Josie replied, still staring at the young man she had a secret crush on while she was in Lagos. "You wouldn't happen to have time for a quick coffee and a chat, would you?"

Josie snapped out of her reverie and realising that he was actually holding her hand, snatched it back.

"I'm sorry. Unfortunately, I have an appointment with a friend of mine, and I am already running late."

She wanted to get away as soon as possible before he asked for her phone number, which she had no intention of giving him. However, at the same time, she was curious to know whether he had secured the diplomatic job he craved so much. She remembered how he used to tell them that his greatest ambition was to work with the Ministry of Foreign Affairs and ultimately be posted outside Nigeria. She and Bosede used to make fun of him about his unbridled diplomatic ambition and how he viewed it as a stepping stone into Nigerian politics.

"So Akin, did you eventually get the job with the Ministry of Foreign Affairs?"

"Of course, I did. Why do you think I am here? I am currently working at the Nigerian High Commission as the Senior Assistant to the Legal Attaché," he replied in that cocky manner which she found rather irritating.

"I must say that I am surprised. How did you get such a role so quickly? If I remember correctly, you were just rounding up your internship at a law firm when Bosede and I were about to graduate. That was…"

"Two years ago, to be precise," he butted in. "My dear, like I told you, in Nigeria, you just need to know the right people, have the right connections, and you will find yourself climbing up the ladder at lightning speed. I guess it is the same in most countries. Anyway, are you going to change your mind about coffee?" he asked again branding a smug smile.

"Like I said, I am meeting a friend of mine who happens to be getting married next month. Oh, there she is."

Josie spotted Lilly Ann waving in the distance.

"Well, it was nice seeing you again. I hope you enjoy your stay here," Josie said as she hurried away, giving the young man no chance for further conversation.

To be honest, she was not sure she wanted to see him again. Even though Josie liked him, she could barely stand his cocky arrogance.

By the time she reached the café, Josie was almost out of breath.

"So, who was the handsome young man I saw you talking to?" Lilly Ann asked as they sat down.

"Just a guy I met when I was in Nigeria. I am sure I told you about him. In fact, I remember boring you with stories about how he used to take me and BA to those crazy Nigerian parties that lasted all night."

"Oh, don't tell me, is that the one and only Mr Akin?" They both burst out in laughter.

After the waiter had taken their orders, Josie noticed that Lilly Ann was looking very serious.

"Josie, I need you to tell me the truth. Why don't you want to be my chief bridesmaid? I always thought that you would be my chief bridesmaid and I would be yours. I thought you felt the same way too, but I was obviously wrong!"

"Oh Lilly, not this again!" Josie exclaimed. "I thought I explained everything the last time we spoke?"

"Well, I was not satisfied with your explanation. I got the feeling that there was more to it. Come on Josie, we've known each other for ages, and I know when you're not telling me something."

"I came here today to take my mind off things, and here you are trying to mess up my day. Maybe this meeting wasn't a good idea after all," Josie retorted as she made to get up and leave.

Lilly Ann knew her friend was still nursing the wounds of her past, and though she was sorry for being insensitive to her feelings, Lilly knew that one day, like it or not, Josie would have to stop running and face her fears head-on.

"Okay Josie, I am sorry. I really am. You are like a sister to me; I would never do anything to intentionally hurt you. I just want you to be real with me. Anyway, I promise not to harass you anymore, and I also want you to know that I am grateful that at least you agreed to be one of my bridesmaids," Lilly Ann smiled.

"It's alright, Lilly. Let's just forget the last twenty minutes ever happened and try and enjoy the rest of our time together."

With a truce secured, the friends shared a smile. However, Lilly was still keen to keep the conversation flowing.

"Do you know what? For a while, I actually thought the reason you didn't want to be my chief was because I chose to marry Peter instead of your brother."

"Why would you think that?" Josie chuckled. "Well, to be fair when I learnt you were seeing Peter Rowe, it did feel a bit awkward. It was like you had betrayed my brother. However, after speaking to him, he seemed perfectly okay. In fact, he said he was not ready to settle down, and that he had expressed this to you. Bruce also said that he had encouraged the relationship between you and Pete. So, I am truly very happy for you."

Time flew by, and before they knew it, it was almost six o'clock in the evening. Josie walked Lilly Ann to the underground station to catch a train to Putney, where she planned to meet up with her cousin and some of her fiancé's friends.

Peter and Lilly Ann had bought a property in Putney which needed refurbishing, but since he was currently on a work-related trip to Singapore and was not expected back until the week of the wedding, he had asked a few trusted friends to help get the house ready before the special day. Also, he had asked his parents, who lived up in Edinburgh, to meet up with the Burtons every now and then to discuss the modalities and logistics of the upcoming wedding and to ensure that everything was in place by the time he came back from his trip.

Eventually, the two friends said their goodbyes. Lilly Ann jumped on the train and Josie made her way back home.

Josie had a bounce in her step as she walked through the front door, a mood change her parents welcomed, but they wondered how long it would last. The last few months had been like a rollercoaster ride when it came to their daughter. There were days when she reminded them of the chirpy, loving girl they had always known. But then there were others when she turned into an almost unbearable, taciturn woman, so hard to understand and difficult to reach out to.

Meanwhile, Bruce was doing all he could to make sure his sister was happy. Since moving out of the family house, he had tried, to no avail, to persuade her to visit him, hoping it might help take things off her mind a little. Whenever Bruce visited, he noticed that Josie was either busy writing or had her eyes glued to her laptop. She hardly ever engaged in conversation unless it had something to do with some form of abuse or another. Josie had become totally immersed in fighting for this cause, and even though he was proud of her, he couldn't help but feel that it was not healthy. But how could he tell her without upsetting her?

The Burtons and the Kimberleys had known each other since their children were toddlers and had always done things together. Lilly Ann's wedding would be no different, even though deep down inside both families wished she was getting married to Bruce.

As the day drew closer, Josie threw herself into helping Lilly Ann with preparations; going from one shop to the other, making purchases and returning unwanted items. And it came as no surprise that Lilly Ann's brother Drake was the ring bearer, and Daphne and Lois Kimberley were both flower girls.

The preparations for the wedding went up a notch when Peter came back from his trip to the Far East, arriving just in time for the dress rehearsal at the Church, where the officiating Minister just happened to be a family friend of the Burtons.

10
Shaken

Two weeks had passed since the wedding.

Josie was working on her laptop as usual when she got a call from Mrs Pearce reminding her that Leah would be going out with Michael Jr and Dora May. Josie remembered giving her approval the day she gave their presents to her daughter, but she did not remember agreeing on a date. It dawned on Josie that as long as Carol was Leah's foster mother, there were some decisions she could not oppose, and she respected that.

"Thank you for letting me know. Is it okay if I pay for the outing?" Josie appreciated Mrs Pearce telling her even though she didn't really have to, but she definitely did not want anyone giving her daughter handouts.

"My dear, it's okay. The children have what they need."

"Thank you so much for all the help and support," Josie replied reluctantly, having no choice but to swallow her unvoiced pride. "I don't know what would have become of Leah if you had not stepped in when you did. I owe you a debt of gratitude."

"It has been a pleasure looking after Leah. Even though she

is like a daughter to me, seeing both of you together makes me so happy. I guess we have my dear friends, Kathleen and her sister, to thank for that."

"It seems I am indebted to quite a few people for being there when it looked like all was over. Thank you so much. When all this is over, I am going to write a book about my experience, a warning to all the innocent, naive and gullible young girls out there. Please, if you don't mind, can you call me when Leah and Emily get back. I would personally like to thank Dora May and Michael Jr."

"Not to worry my dear, I most certainly will."

After talking to Mrs Pearce, Josie went downstairs to speak to her mother who had just gotten back from the local Samaritan Charity shop, where she volunteered twice a week. She found her ruminating in the garage.

"Hi mum, what are you doing in here?" Josie noticed the distant look in her mother's eyes.

"Oh, Josie I didn't hear you come in," Angela exclaimed, looking startled. "I can't seem to find my garden gloves. I am sure I left them here last week. Your father must have moved them. He is always pottering around here."

"Mum, let me help."

After an exhaustive forty minutes, Angela's garden gloves were nowhere to be found. Josie knew her mother really wanted to do some work in the garden, so she volunteered to pop out and get her a new pair from the supermarket.

"You don't need to do that. I can wait till your father gets back. I am sure he will remember where he stuffed them."

"Okay mum, if you insist. By the way, I just got off the phone with Mrs Pearce. She told me that Dora May and Michael Jr were coming over to her house to take Leah out, and wanted to ask if it was alright."

"Ah, that was nice of her."

"My sentiments exactly, especially as she didn't have to."

"Carol is a wonderful woman, and she looked after Leah like her own daughter. I doubt if I could have done a better job myself," Angela replied.

"I am so grateful to her. Can you imagine what could have happened to Leah if Mrs Pearce hadn't run into her at the station? Talking about being in the right place at the right time!"

Josie lay on the couch thinking about where she and Leah would spend the long school holiday, and was still in a pensive mood when her mother walked in.

Angela had seen that look before, and for some random reason, she began to wonder if her daughter had started thinking about why they gave Leah to the Dolands in the first place. The silence was killing her, and just as she was about to interrupt her daughter's thoughts, Josie looked at her.

"What's for dinner, mum?"

Angela was so relieved that she just blurted out what came to her lips.

"Roast potatoes and braised steak. Is that still your favourite dish?"

"It sure is!" Josie exclaimed. "Do you need any help?"

"Now that you ask, would you mind picking up some brussels sprouts from the supermarket, as well as a nice bottle of red wine. Do you know what? Let me write you a list so that I don't leave anything out."

Josie ran upstairs to grab her purse and when she was ready her mum handed her the list and advised her to take the car so that she would not end up having to carry heavy shopping bags on the bus.

Once Josie had left for the supermarket, it crossed Angela's mind to call Carol. She wanted to find out what her plans were for the upcoming holiday. She thought it might be nice for both families to go away together. It would give Josie and her daughter a fantastic opportunity to get to know each other more, and it would also give Daphne and Lois a chance to get to know Leah and Carol's daughter, Emily. So, she took out her mobile phone from her apron pocket and was about to call Carol when it suddenly started ringing. It was not a number she knew, and even though she tried to ignore the call, Angela's curiosity finally got the better of her.

"Hello. Hello."

Angela could hear a lot of noise in the background and then she heard someone barking out orders. It sounded bizarre.

"Who is this?" Angela shouted.

She heard what sounded like a gunshot, then the phone went dead. Angela stood there, her heart pounding as she trembled. She tried calling the number several times, but the line was dead. Angela ran into the living room and switched on the television. It was the same breaking news on almost every news channel.

There had been a terrorist attack at the underground station near the supermarket; the same supermarket she had sent her daughter to. She tried calling Josie, and to her relief, Josie picked up the phone. Josie was screaming and crying on the other end of the line.

"What's the matter? Where are you?" Angela shouted down the line.
"Mum, I am under a table in a restaurant on the High Street. There is an ongoing standoff between the police and another gang. Some are saying that it is a terrorist attack. I can't talk

anymore in case they hear me. Please pray, I am so scared and..." There was an eerie silence as her daughter's voice was abruptly cut off.

Josie, along with some others caught up in the shootings, was still hiding under the table when the police came in and escorted them to the designated safe areas. Josie was shaking all over. Her legs felt so stiff, she could hardly stand up and walk. Eventually, she was assisted by a policewoman carrying a heavy gun and a truncheon. Josie just about managed to remember where she parked her car and was able to direct the kind officer who was helping her.

"Are you sure you are alright to drive?" the officer asked. "Or is there someone you can call to come and get you?"
"I will be fine. I just need some time to gather myself together," Josie replied.
"Okay. You will be directed through the back exit to avoid the High Street." the policewoman advised.
"Thank you, officer. I feel much better now," Josie flashed a timid smile.

Josie waited for about twenty minutes before inserting the key into the ignition. Her hands were still shaking, her palms were sweaty. If only she had gone home when she finished the supermarket shopping, if only she hadn't decided to get that mocha from Pret a Manger. Josie lowered her head on to the steering and started crying. She remembered hearing gunshots as she was about to exit the café. How her cup of mocha dropped out of her hands and how everyone started shouting, "Get down, get down!" She didn't need anyone to tell her that something was wrong, she hit the floor and scrambled under the table for safety.

By the time Josie drove out of the supermarket car park's back exit, she couldn't wait to run into her mother's loving arms.

As she got home, she jumped out of the car, ran into the house and collapsed in the hallway, tears flowing from her eyes. Her mother, whose eyes were glued to the television watching the day's events unfold, heard her daughter come in, rushed to the door and cradled her on the floor. Angela didn't ask any questions, she didn't say a word. She simply breathed a sigh of relief as she held Josie's shaking body in her arms and rocked her like a baby. Thoughts of her daughter's past popped into her mind. She tried to get rid of them but to no avail. Angela was still struggling with these persisting, negative thoughts when she heard her daughter's voice.

"Mum, why do bad things always seem to happen to me? Is there something wrong with me?

It was as if Josie had read her mother's mind.

"What is that supposed to mean? Of course, there is nothing wrong with you," Angela tried to assure her daughter.
"But I always seem to be in the wrong place at the wrong time. It happened at St Magdalene's, it happened at the University of Lagos, it happened when Bosede and I were in the Republic of Benin, and now it's happening again."
"Josie, take a look on the bright side. Even if you were right, and I don't think you are, at least you have always come out unscathed."
"Unscathed! Mum, is that what you call this?"

Angela could sense the conversation going downhill. She needed to think of something and fast.

"How about we get you off the floor and I make you a hot cup of chocolate?"
"Thanks, mum, but I don't want anything right now. Can I watch the news and see what is happening?"
"If that is what you want my dear."

She helped her daughter up, and they both walked to the living room, sat on the couch and watched the news.

"So, it's confirmed, the attack was terror-related!" Josie exclaimed, echoing the words of the newscaster. "What is wrong with these people; what do they actually want? I just don't get it!"
"Well, welcome to the real world," Angela said, shaking her head. "Personally, I think it has to do with hate, a lack of understanding of cultures and traditions, and a refusal to integrate with the larger society."

Sleep finally caught up with Josie as she listened to updates of the day's terrorist attack, and when she woke up, all she wanted to do was erase everything that had happened earlier on. Suddenly Josie jumped up and grabbed her phone. Mrs Pearce was meant to have called her once the children came back from the park, but there was no missed call. She needed to know that Leah and the other children were safe.

Josie called Mrs Pearce several times, but there was no response. She began to panic as all kinds of thoughts ran through her mind. She would never forgive herself if anything happened to her Leah. Just as Josie was about to call again, her phone rang. It was Mrs Pearce!

"Oh, hello Mrs Pearce, I am so sorry to disturb you, but after everything that happened on the High Street earlier on today, I just wanted to find out if the children came back safely."
"Yes, they did. The children said they had a lovely time. However, they all came back hungry, so I am making them something to eat. By the way, what happened on the High Street?" Carol asked, sounding a bit confused.

"You didn't hear? Well, there was an alleged terrorist attack."

"Really? My television has been off all day, mainly because I have been busy pottering in the garden. I will endeavour to catch up on the news once the Doland children have gone home, and Leah and Emily are in bed."

"Thank you so much!"

"Don't be silly Josie, the pleasure is all mine. Give my love to your mother."

"I will. Bye for now."

Josie heaved a sigh of relief as she dropped the phone.

11

Holiday Preps

The judge had announced that the court would recess from the last week of July till the first week of September, which according to the Kimberley family lawyer, Mr Salmon Goldberg would afford them ample time to work and liaise with the Office of the Prosecutor, especially as Josie had waived her right to an anonymous hearing, insisting that she wanted to face Michael Doland in court.

Josie was still in the process of carefully compiling her facts as she did not want to leave any stone unturned. But once her dossier on Michael was ready, she planned to hand it over to Mr Goldberg who in turn would forward it to the Prosecutor's office. Josie was prepared to tell anyone willing to listen all about what had happened. She had nothing to hide.

Away from the hustle and bustle of the court case preparations, Josie had started planning for their family holiday. She still wasn't sure about the destination or departure date, even though her mum had hinted that it would be either Dubai or Tenerife, but really, she couldn't be bothered. Just being with Leah was all that mattered to her. It was the first holiday that she was going to spend with her daughter and Josie was determined to make it a memorable one.

In her excitement, she had gone on a shopping spree buying clothes and other things for both Leah and Emily. Mrs Pearce's daughter had been like a sister to Leah; both of them did almost everything together, and Josie secretly dreaded what might happen once she gained full custody of her daughter. "Well, we will cross that bridge when we get there," Josie sighed.

Daphne and Lois were due back from their Frankfurt school trip the next day, and their mother had already tidied their bedrooms. Angela changed the beddings, hoovered the carpet and emptied the bins, ready for their return. She also planned what she was going to cook for them, and of course, she continually reminded her husband not to forget to pick the girls up from the airport. Angela had missed the girls and was super excited to have them back, especially as the house had been rather quiet ever since they left.

Josie had eagerly helped around the house, but she was more excited about the family's upcoming holiday. Out of curiosity, she decided to ask her mum if the arrangements had been finalised. As she approached her mum's room, Josie heard her talking to someone over the phone. She quietly pressed her ear against the door to listen in on the conversation and was soon able to deduce that it was her dad on the other end of the phone. Then just when she was about to walk away, Josie heard her mum exclaim.

"Oh, no! How did that happen?"

Since she couldn't hear what her dad was saying, Josie decided to wait, hoping to catch on to what her parents were discussing. Her attempt was in vain. Finally, when she heard her mum drop the phone, Josie quickly ran towards the staircase and turned so that when her mum opened her door, it would look like she had just walked up the stairs. Josie took a good look at her mother, and seeing no visible sign of anxiety or distress, she concluded that all was well and assumed that if anything unpleasant had happened, her mother would tell her. So, Josie went ahead to ask if her mum had spoken to her friend as promised.

"Mum have you spoken to Mrs Pearce yet?"
"About what?" Angela asked, looking distracted.
"Mum, what's the matter?"
"I just spoke to your father. Unfortunately, he won't be joining us for dinner tonight. A colleague of his was rushed to the hospital, and your father's gone to pay him a visit."
"Did he tell you what happened?"
"Not really. Just that the man, who is married with three children, had a history of diabetes. Let us just pray that he gets well soon."
"Oh, so sorry to hear that."

Josie wasn't too sure if she should still ask about the holiday, and was about to go back downstairs when her mother tapped her on the shoulder.

"Josie, was there something you wanted to ask me?"
"Oh, I just wanted to find out if you and Mrs Pearce had finalised the holiday arrangements. We are still going together, right?"

Josie followed her mum back into the room and helped straighten the bedsheets while continuing the conversation.

"I actually spoke to Carol earlier, and she promised to call me back later on in the evening. As things stand, I am pretty sure we will all be going on holiday together. She did, however, say that even if she couldn't make it, Leah definitely would."

"I would really prefer that we all went together though."

"I know this holiday means a lot to you, but let us wait and see?"

"Okay, mum. I just think it will help take my mind off the impending court case and more importantly allow me to spend precious time with my daughter. She is growing up so fast."

"I understand, and I believe everything will work out well."

After talking to her mum, Josie went to her room and decided to blog about her upcoming holiday, her impending court appearance, her custody battle and her future intentions. She was still blogging when her father came home. Knowing his routine, she knew he would go straight up to his room, change and wash his hands and face before coming back downstairs and inevitably relaxing in his chair with a cup of coffee. Her dad was a caffeine addict, just like grandad.

Josie went downstairs, greeted her dad, who was talking to her mum and poured herself some tomato juice before sitting down to listen to the events of her dad's exciting evening. He told them how it all happened so suddenly; how he was preparing for his last meeting of the day when his secretary alerted him to what had happened on the office floor.

"That was when I called to let you know that I wasn't going to make dinner."

"Your visit obviously didn't last that long because you are back a lot earlier than I thought," Angela remarked.

"Well, when we got to the hospital, we were told that he had been taken to the Intensive Care Unit as the doctors feared he was about to go into a diabetic coma."

"Has his wife been notified?" Josie asked, noticing how the saga had put her father in a pensive mood.

"Yes, she has. After leaving the hospital, a few of us went to see her. Luckily her grown-up daughter was visiting, which made the unpleasant task of telling her about her husband a bit easier. Surprisingly, they didn't look too surprised. It was as if they were expecting something to happen."

"I didn't know that diabetes was such a deadly disease. I thought it could be controlled?" Josie said, looking concerned.

"Well, from my little understanding, as long as you take your medication as directed, stick to the prescribed meal plan, exercise regularly and try and stay stress-free, it normally helps."

"I have heard that in extreme cases, it can lead to amputation of the limbs," Angela added.

Josie shuddered. She wanted to change the topic but did not want to come across as unsympathetic. Fortunately, her mum's phone rang. It was from Mrs Pearce.

"Hello, Carol, how are you?"

"I am very well, thank you. Sorry about earlier on, I had a few things I needed to sort out. Anyway, I have scanned through some of the holiday brochures I picked up, and I think we need to finalise things quickly as fares seem to be going up daily."

"Alright, do you mind if I call you back in about thirty minutes, we're just in the middle of a family discussion."

"That's perfectly fine," Carol replied.

As Angela put down the phone, she found herself looking into prying eyes.

"It was Carol," she said, as John and Josie stared at her.

"And?" her husband probed wearing a silly smile.

"Well, she said the fares are going up, so we need to finalise…"

"But I thought both of you had already wrapped this up,"

John interrupted. "All I was waiting for were the destination, flight and hotel details."

"I agree, but I don't really want to burden Carol in any way."

"What is that supposed to mean?" John asked.

"Well, I thought that since we suggested the holiday, and as a way to say thank you for everything the Pearces have done, we should pay for all their expenses."

"Of course," John bellowed. "Is that what's causing the delay?"

"Dad, mum," Josie interjected. "Is it okay if I pay for Emily and Leah?"

"My dear, I am not sure about that." Then turning to her husband asked, "John, have you decided where we are going yet?"

"I thought you said we were going to Tenerife," John said, looking surprised.

"Alright then, I will talk to Carol, and we should hopefully have it all sorted out before the end of the day."

It turned out that Angela's fears were unwarranted. Her conversation with Carol went quite well. Within an hour, everything was in place. They had decided on the destination, the hotel and the date, and Carol even agreed for Josie to pay for Leah and Emily.

The smile on Angela's face when she dropped the phone said it all. Tenerife was the destination and the fourth of August, which was barely two weeks away, was departure day. All in all, everything had worked out better than she could have planned. The only downside was that, due to a prior business commitment, John would have to fly into Tenerife a day later.

12

Quality Time

On the fourth of August as Angela, Carol and the girls made their way to the airport, John received a call from the Crown Prosecutor's office.

A date had been fixed for the first hearing of the case; R vs Michael Doland. The appearance and jury selection were set for the same day in the second week of September. He immediately called his wife and told her about the latest update and asked her to pass the news on to their daughter.

It was a strange feeling, but Josie was quietly pleased. "Finally, this rigmarole will be over, and everyone can get on with their lives," she thought. For her, it was the beginning and the end of all her past, present and future problems. The strength of her resolve made her more determined than ever to face whatever the defence threw at her. She was a woman on a mission, and she intended to make her day in court count. She would never be a victim again!

They arrived at the airport way earlier than expected, and after checking in and going through security, there was ample time to sit down for breakfast. Afterwards, they slowly made their way to the departure lounge. Daphne, Lois, Emily and Leah were having so much fun. They skipped all over the place and couldn't stop giggling. It was as if they were infused with contagious excitement. Seeing the way the four girls got along brought a smile to Josie's face, it was exactly how she wanted it to be.

Boarding was smooth as Angela had wisely booked premium-class tickets, and before too long they were on their way to Tenerife. Thirty minutes into the flight and most of the passengers were snoring, but the Kimberleys and the Pearces were still wide awake.

Josie suddenly remembered that she hadn't called her brother from the airport as planned. Apart from giving him their flight details, she also wanted to confirm if Bruce was still going to meet up with them in Tenerife as previously arranged.

"Oh well, I'll just have to call him when we touch down", Josie muttered to herself.

Seeing the smiles on the girls faces and watching her mum and Mrs Pearce chatting away gave Josie a soothing, satisfying feeling.

"If only every day could be like this", she thought.

Josie had recently found some more information which she wanted to share with her followers, so she decided to make use of her 'alone' time by updating her blog. She pulled out her iPad and started typing away. She was so engrossed that the captain's announcement caught her totally by surprise.

"Ladies and gentlemen, this is your captain speaking. As we start our descent, please make sure your seat backs and tray tables are in their upright position. Make sure your seat belt is securely fastened, and all carry-on luggage is stowed underneath the seat in front of you or in the overhead bins. Thank you."

Still looking bewildered, Josie adjusted her seat and fastened her seat belt. It was hard to believe that she had spent the last three hours blogging.

Finally, the wheels touched the tarmac, and as the plane taxied to the gate, the captain's cheery voice came booming over the speakers once again.

"Ladies and gentlemen, welcome to Tenerife South Airport. Local time is 11:38, and the temperature is approximately 28°C.

For your safety and comfort, please remain seated with your seat belt fastened until the Fasten Seat Belt sign goes off. This will indicate that we have parked at the gate and that it is safe for you to move about. Please check around your seat for any personal belongings you may have brought on board with you and please use caution when opening the overhead bins, as items may have shifted around during the flight.

If you require deplaning assistance, please remain in your seat until all other passengers have disembarked. One of our crew members will then be pleased to assist you.

On behalf of the Airline, myself and the entire crew, I'd like to thank you for joining us on this trip, and we look forward to seeing you onboard again sometime soon. Have a pleasant stay."

The plane finally came to a halt, and the girls excitedly jumped out of their seats. Angela and Carol handed them their luggage, and they all made their way to the plane exit door closest to them.

Due to two other flights landing at about the same time as theirs, the queues in the immigration hall were unusually long, but that was not enough to dampen the girls' excitement. Daphne, Lois, Emily and Leah all sang along to their favourite tunes, and when they finally got into the reserved seven-seater SUV, Angela, Carol and Josie had to plead with them to take their voices down a notch.

Josie jumped behind the wheel and set the satnav to take them to the villa located near the northern coastline. It was the same one the Kimberley family stayed in the last time they came to Tenerife, and it held precious, loving memories, but when Josie pulled up in front of the villa everyone, including the girls, were stunned into silence. It had recently been renovated, and it was indeed a beauty to behold.

Inside oozed with quality and style. The modern interiors blended perfectly with the classic furniture, the five delicately designed double bedrooms were each fitted with luxury en suite bathrooms and the beautiful open plan kitchen which featured a large island, was kitted out with top-end kitchenware. Outside did not disappoint either. There was a fabulous Mediterranean-designed garden, a sparkling infinity swimming pool and lots and lots of space.

After taking in the exquisite scenery, they all went to their rooms; Mrs Pearce and her daughter in one, Josie and Leah in another, Angela was in the Master bedroom, Lois and Daphne shared the room beside the Master while the last one was reserved for Bruce if he was able to make it down. They unpacked their cases before scampering to the kitchen where they microwaved, dished and hungrily gobbled down the frozen packaged meals that Angela had picked up from her local deli.

When they finished, Josie and Leah cleared the table while Carol loaded the dishwasher, and by the time they were done, it was almost nine o'clock local time. So, they switched on the television and sat down to listen to the news. There was nothing new; the usual political brouhaha in Europe, the America/China trade war and the upcoming US primaries. One by one, as the not so new news unravelled, they all fell asleep only to be awakened by the sound of a low flying plane. When the noise finally faded into the distance, they all said their goodnights and went to sleep.

It was the first time since their separation that Josie and Leah had shared the same room. At first, Josie was apprehensive, not knowing what to do or say. But Leah had no such fears. She was just happy to be with her real mum.

"I love you so much, and I am glad that you are my mum."

Tears in her eyes, Josie looked nonplussed, but eventually took her daughter in her arms and held her close to her bosom.

"I love you too little one, and I am so sorry for everything I put you through."
"Mum, you have been through a lot too, and I know now that if not for what happened things would have been different. It wasn't your fault."
"But I should have been there to protect you, and I wasn't."
"That's all in the past, mum. We are together now. That is all that matters."

They sat on the bed and talked into the early hours of the morning. Josie told Leah about the upcoming court case, and as she did, she could see the worried look in her daughter's eyes.

"Mum, are you nervous?"
"In all honesty, not really," Josie replied. "With all the information I have gathered, I believe I am ready to take the stand, and as I tell my side of the story, I look forward to seeing Michael and his mother squirm."
"I want to testify in court too," Leah whispered. "Michael, Dora and I discussed it the last time we met up, and they

encouraged me to do it."

"Hmm, I am not too sure about that, my dear. You can give evidence, but it definitely will not be in the courtroom, in front of the whole world. Defence lawyers can be ruthless. They know how to twist facts, and I'm sure if given a chance the Doland lawyer will do everything within his power to make you look like a liar."

"Well, if he does that to me, I will just look at the judge like this and start crying," Leah pulled a sad-looking face that made Josie laugh. "I know this look will win the sympathy of the judge and members of the jury," Leah concluded before bursting into laughter herself.

"Oh my God, look at the time. It's almost three o'clock. We need to get some sleep, little one."

"Okay mummy. Will you tuck me in please?"

"Of course. Good night my darling. Sleep peacefully," Josie cooed as she covered her daughter with the duvet.

"Good night, mummy. I love you."

"I love you too, my dear."

Josie lay awake till about five as she reminisced on some of the things she and her daughter had been through before finally drifting off to sleep.

"Wakey, wakey, mummy!"

She could smell the scent of fresh coffee beans and hear a sweet voice singing in the background. Was she dreaming? Josie felt a gentle tap on her shoulder, and through half-closed eyes, she saw her daughter holding a tray. Josie slowly sat up.

"Thank you, Leah. What time is it?" Josie asked as she took a sip of the fresh coffee."

"It is almost ten o'clock."

"What!" Josie exclaimed.

She jumped out of bed and ran straight into the bathroom. As the designated driver, the last thing she wanted to do was let the 'crew' down.

13
The Hunch

The group had come up with an itinerary of what to do and where to visit on each day of the holiday. There was also a rota for who would do the cleaning and the washing up. Since Josie's cooking skills were limited to frying plantain and boiling eggs, something she learnt while she was in Lagos, all the cooking was left to Angela and Carol. So, it was a good thing she had volunteered to do the driving.

That afternoon, as she drove through town, Josie started feeling restless. It was a feeling she had felt before, and it almost always meant that something unpleasant was going to happen. Josie tried to shake it off but couldn't, and if she hadn't heard Daphne, Lois and Emily screaming she would have run into a stationary vehicle. Josie pulled over; her hands were shaking. After a brief second, she turned around to find everyone gazing at her with some disquiet.

"Mummy, what's the matter? Are you alright?" Leah asked in a confused but gentle voice.
"I'm okay," Josie replied. "It's just that since waking up this morning I keep having these flashbacks as if something

terrible is about to happen, but I can't quite place my finger on it."

Suddenly Josie looked at her mother.

"Mum, have you heard from dad or Bruce yet?"
"Not yet, but I am sure they are fine. Leah told us you did not sleep till five this morning. Maybe you should have rested a bit more, especially as you knew you would be driving," her mum remonstrated.
"Mum, this has nothing to do with my sleeping or the lack of it. All I am asking is for you to call dad or Bruce and make sure they are okay. That's all."
"Maybe we should go back to the villa," Carol interjected.

Josie pulled up in front of the villa and stayed in her seat, door ajar, while the others went inside. Lost in thought, she did not notice Emily and Leah walk round to where she was sitting. They took her hands and looking sheepishly, tried to reassure her in their own little way. Josie smiled at them timidly, got out of the car and all three of them walked into the villa, hand in hand.

On getting inside, Josie turned on the television. The news was on, and the headline was that a suspected drunken pilot had been escorted off a plane. Now, every eye was glued to the screen. Interestingly, it had also been discovered that a passenger had somehow managed to breach security and board the same aircraft, and as a result, all the passengers had been asked to calmly disembark while the situation was resolved. However, from the pictures being shown, there seemed to be some commotion.

That was when it occurred to Josie that her dad was scheduled to be on that flight. She looked at her mother and saw the visible panic on her face. Angela frantically picked up the phone and tried calling her husband. There was no answer. At the same time, Josie called Bruce to find out if he was aware of what was going on at the airport, but his phone went straight to his voice mail. Not knowing what to do next, they all continued to watch the breaking news, and before their very eyes, a fight broke out between one of the passengers and a member of the airport staff. The police swiftly moved in and escorted both men to a corner to determine the cause of the fracas. That's when Lois pointed to the television, shouting excitedly.

"Look, that's daddy on his phone. It's daddy!"
"Indeed, it is!" Angela exclaimed, relieved. Then her phone rang.
"John, are you alright? You won't believe it, but your face is on the news right now."
"I am fine. We have been advised that it is a minor situation that should be settled soon and that we should be boarding again within the hour. So, there is nothing to worry about."
"Alright, but please keep us posted. Let us know when you board and before you take off."
"I will, darling. How is everyone over there?"
"Well, we are all enjoying the lovely weather. Just hurry up and get yourself over here."
"Okay," John chuckled and dropped the phone.

Everyone turned to look at Josie.

"Why are you all looking at me?" she asked.
"Well, it looks like your feeling was justified," Carol responded. "Let us thank God that it was not a terrorist attack."
"Phew, now that's over can we still go to the beach?" Daphne asked, jumping excitedly to her feet, looking at her mum and Josie.

Daphne's request was met with an awkward silence. Josie was in no frame of mind to drive, and without her driving, they were not going anywhere.

"I am sorry Daphne, but I think I need to rest a bit," Josie finally replied. "I guess we might have to wait till dad arrives, either today or tomorrow."
"Okay then," Daphne said, slumping back into the chair.

It was almost time for lunch anyway, so Angela and Carol popped into the kitchen to rustle up something to eat. Emily and Leah followed to help out, while Lois and Daphne just sat there looking at their sister, partly annoyed that she was the sole reason why they were stuck indoors. However, when they saw her drift off, they realised that she must have been exhausted. So as not to disturb her, Daphne quietly switched off the television, and both she and Lois joined the rest of the family in the kitchen.

About two hours later, while they were still seated at the dining table, Angela's phone rang. It was John calling to let her know that he had boarded the plane and that the flight was scheduled to arrive in Tenerife at 5:00pm local time.

John was used to the island, having been there on several occasions for business and pleasure. So, Angela wasn't too concerned when he told her that he would take a taxi to the villa. Knowing that John was finally on his way had lightened the atmosphere. Everyone suddenly seemed relaxed, and after lunch, since it was such a beautiful day, they all went into the garden to enjoy the scenery, play on the swings and feed the fish before dozing off on the chaise lounges in the garden shade.

Meanwhile, in England, John's British Airways flight to Tenerife took off as scheduled and touched down at Tenerife Sur approximately four hours later. As soon as he cleared his baggage from the arrival hall, he made his way to the taxi point on the west side of the airport. In no time, Juan, the taxi driver, helped John load his luggage into the boot, and they were off to the villa. On their way, John tried calling Angela, and when she didn't pick up, he called Josie instead.

"Hi dad, where are you?" Josie asked excitedly.
"I am on my way to the villa. I called your mum, but she didn't pick up."
"Mum is relaxing in the garden. I think she might be sleeping. Let me go and check."
"Not to worry. I will be there soon, anyway."
"Alright, see you soon then."

Josie did not notice that her mum was standing behind her and was startled when she heard her voice.

"Josie, was that your dad?"
"Yes, mum. I thought you were sleeping in the garden and dad said I shouldn't disturb you. Anyway, he is on his way and should be here soon."
"Okay, I will make something for him to eat. I am sure he will be famished." Angela dashed to the kitchen.

Daphne and Lois jumped on their father as he walked through the front door. When he finally managed to get the girls off him, he walked over to Emily and Leah, who were both smiling excitedly, and gave them both a cuddle, before giving Carol a hug. Finally, he walked over to Josie and his wife and embraced them warmly then he gave Angela a peck on the lips.

"Well, thank you all for making me feel like royalty. Guess what? As a treat, I would like to take us all out to eat."
"Yippee!" the girls chorused as they held hands and jumped around in a circle.
"But John," Angela began, "I have already made you something to eat."

"Never mind my dear, I'm sure that can wait till tomorrow," John replied winking at his not so chuffed wife.

"I made a reservation for this evening at The El Rincon de Juan Carlos Restaurant before I left London. A colleague of mine recommended it and guaranteed that we would not be disappointed."

So, they got ready and jumped into the car. Josie was glad she didn't have to drive. At least from now on, she would actually be able to enjoy the scenery instead of having to think about navigating along winding roads that seemed to curve endlessly.

The décor and the relaxed ambience of the restaurant were simply amazing. They were ushered to their table, and as soon as they were seated, the maître d'hôtel was at hand to take their orders. John graciously interpreted what was on the menu to the younger ones who were not so familiar with the Spanish dishes.

To everyone's surprise, while they waited for their drinks, a gentleman in a white top came to greet John. He introduced himself as the owner of the restaurant and that John's friend had informed him that they would be dining at the restaurant that evening. He then went on to say that as a welcome gesture to their great island, dinner was on the house. John tried to object, but the owner insisted. Then before John could create a scene, two musicians playing the accordion came to their table and started serenading them. Emily and Leah immediately started clapping while Lois and Daphne waved their hands to the music. The accordionists played by the table until their food was served.

The food was simply delicious, and when they finally finished, the leftovers were packed in stylish takeaway boxes. They bade the owner goodnight and John left a hefty tip for the waiters who had simply been excellent all night.

When John pulled up in front of the villa, they all tiredly alighted from the car, trudged up the steps to the front door and made their way straight to bed.

14
The Climb

J osie woke up early and jumped into the bathroom. She planned to quickly get ready so she could help her mum and Mrs Pearce out with breakfast. However, while having a shower, Josie was surprised to hear her parents talking next door. Her mother's voice sounded much louder than usual, so she knew something wasn't right. Josie turned off the shower, put her ear against the wall and tried to listen to their muffled voices. She wasn't sure, but she thought she heard her dad say something like, "…but, what did you expect me to do? When he comes tomorrow, you and Josie can decide on what to say to him."

She struggled to make any sense of what her dad was referring to, and why her name had even come up in the conversation in the first place. Now Josie was even more curious. With her ear still firmly against the wall, she heard her mum's voice, it was a lot clearer than her dad's.

"John, have you thought about Josie's reaction? Seeing that girl with her brother might reopen old wounds."
"Angela, in case you haven't noticed, your daughter is not the same vulnerable little girl she was at St. Magdalene's."

"Well, I sincerely hope Bruce knows what he is doing because I would not want to be in his shoes when Josie confronts him. What nonsense!"

"Angela, you need to take it easy."

Then Josie heard a door slam and concluded that it was her mother leaving the room. She quickly finished off in the bathroom and got dressed. Then she woke Leah up, told her to get ready and come downstairs for breakfast.

Angela and Carol were in the middle of laying the table for breakfast when Josie walked into the kitchen.

"Good morning mum, good morning Mrs Pearce. Is there anything I can help with?"

"Good morning, my dear. It's nice to see you up nice and early and sounding so chirpy," Angela said, almost sounding sarcastic.

Carol smiled and handed Josie the cereal bowls.

By the time breakfast was ready, everyone, including John, was seated at the table and after saying grace, they all pounced on the food. It was evident that the enormous meal they ate the night before had long digested. However, it was still a talking point over breakfast, especially the amazing hospitality.

After breakfast, they all went back upstairs and packed for the long day ahead. Angela and Carol filled two baskets with food and drinks and reminded everyone to pack their swimming gear as they planned on having a beach picnic after the ride on the Teide Cableway.

Try as she might, Josie could not get what she overheard out of her head. She did not know who her brother was bringing or what he planned to do, but for her mother to object so vehemently, she knew it was serious, and not in a good way.

"Who could it be?" Josie wondered. From the little she heard, it seemed to her that it was someone she knew, someone who she disliked and might have had a tiff with in the past. Now Josie wished she never heard the conversation; the suspense was tearing her up inside. It was going to be hard, but whatever the case she was going to have to try and get through the day without giving anything away. "After all, tomorrow was less than twenty-four hours away," she told herself.

To make the day more enjoyable, Angela had asked a friend to be their tour guide. Hugh was British, but he had lived on the island for so long that one would never have known. Angela smiled to herself as she remembered how they met.

Six of them had come to Tenerife to celebrate a friend's birthday. It was a fantastic time, and maybe they let their hair down a bit too much. The way they hit the club dance floor and pranced about, one would never have known that they were all married women with grown-up children. So, it came as no surprise when they were approached by some hunks. One of those young men was Hugh. When, at the end of the day, the young men found out the truth they all trudged away disappointingly, except Hugh who seemed to find the scenario rather amusing. Over time, Hugh had become a good friend to John and Angela, and anytime they came to Tenerife, they tried to meet up.

As they alighted from the aerial tramway at the top of Mount Teide, Hugh, himself an avid trekker, made them walk to a place that overlooked Costa Adeje. The houses and apartments they saw from their villa seemed like they were hewn from the side of the hills. They saw the beach line, with all the yachts and fishing boats. The blue sea was serene. They could even see the descent of the road that led to their villa. It was indeed a beautiful spectacle!

The walk from the base camp to the hill was exhausting, and when Hugh said that the plan was to hike up one of the mountains, Carol and Angela decided that they'd had enough. They tried to persuade the girls not to climb but to no avail; Daphne, Lois, Emily and Leah were way too excited to say no. So, Hugh, John, Josie and the girls set off leaving the women behind.

As they started to climb, Hugh noticed the look on Josie's face. Unknown to everyone, she was afraid of heights. The higher they went, the narrower the climbing path became, and the more Josie's anxiety grew. She started to panic, holding on tightly to anything and everything to try and keep her footing. So, Hugh decided to find a safe spot for them to rest and went over to have a quiet word with Josie.

"Josie, are you sure you want to continue or should we turn back?" Hugh asked.

The only reason she had chosen to go along with the mountain climbing was to keep the girls' company, and as she looked at them, she could see that they were trying hard to hide their disappointment.

"No, I should be okay," Josie smiled hesitantly. "However, I may need a bit of assistance along the way."

The girls' faces suddenly lit up again. That was enough encouragement for Josie.

After resting for about fifteen minutes, they continued the climb, and it turned out that Josie needed quite a bit of help. At one stage, both Hugh and her dad had to hold her hands as it seemed as if she was going to topple over. Then Josie decided she would feel safer if she crawled instead. So, even though she looked a sorry sight, she stayed on all fours for most of the climb. What made it even more annoying for Josie was the way everyone else seemed to walk up the mountain as if they were on a leisure stroll. And to add insult to injury, Lois and Daphne couldn't stop laughing as they videoed their sister in her awkward position.

Eventually, they all made it to the top, and for the first time, Josie actually thought it was worth it. The view was absolutely remarkable. Simply breathtaking! They took loads of pictures, some of them a bit daring, and then spent some time meditating and praising God for His awesome wonders.

All the while, Josie was quietly contemplating how she was going to make it down, but it turned out that it was a lot more straightforward. With Hugh patiently guiding her along the narrow paths, the climbing party and a relieved Josie finally made it back to where Angela and Carol were waiting. Understandably, the ladies looked a bit worried, especially as what was meant to be a thirty-minute trek had ended up taking the better part of three hours.

Due to the longer than anticipated cable car ride, and the flashes of lightning in the sky, John suggested that they head back to the villa. It was a wise decision as they were famished and visibly exhausted. Once they got into the car, they all helped themselves to the contents of the picnic baskets, after which Daphne, Lois, Emily and Leah all fell asleep, and when they finally arrived at the villa, everyone except Josie's parents stomped tiredly up the stairs to their bedrooms.

While Angela was busy in the kitchen, John relaxed on the living room couch, sipping a cup of coffee and enjoying his pipe. That was when he felt his phone vibrate. It was a text message from Bruce confirming the time he would arrive in Tenerife the next day. Bruce also told his dad not to bother picking him up from the airport as he had already made the necessary arrangements and that, though he would be staying in the villa with the rest of the family, his guest would be staying with some friends in a nearby lodge. John knew this was his son's attempt at trying to avoid the anticipated confrontation with his sister, who would most likely not approve of his guest.

John sighed, got up, and slowly walked to the kitchen to show his wife their son's message.

> "So, if Bruce knows Josie will not approve, why bring her here in the first place?" Angela quizzed rather loudly. "It is so unlike him."
> "Shh. Keep your voice down. We don't want Josie to hear now, do we?" John warned his wife.
> "Why not?" Angela asked in an argumentative tone. "She is going to find out sooner or later, anyway. I just don't understand what Bruce is doing with a girl who has caused his sister so much grief."

John and Angela were not aware that their daughter was wide awake, sitting at the top of the stairs, listening to them argue. Josie sat still as she tried to think of who her brother's guest might be. Was this person an old friend who had hurt her in the past, she wondered.

"Oh no, could it be Peggy Jones?" she thought. Peggy was the one who, when questioned by the police, had lied that Josie was the one who threw herself at Michael Doland. Even though she couldn't prove it, Josie was convinced that the Dolands had paid

Peggy to lie. So, if Peggy was the one Bruce was bringing along, she would definitely find it hard to forgive him. But Josie was sure Bruce wouldn't do that. She knew that the last thing her beloved brother would do was hurt her.

Josie quietly got up and went to her room, where Leah was sound asleep. As she lay down, it felt as if she was being haunted by Michael Doland's shadow.

"Will I ever be free?" she whispered to herself.

Not wanting to wake her daughter, Josie went into the adjoining cloakroom, closed the door, and cried.

Not long after, Leah woke up; she needed the loo. On her way back to bed, she heard a muffled sound coming from the cloakroom. She tiptoed over, pushed the door open and saw her mum huddled up in a corner, hurriedly wiping her face.

"Mummy, what's the matter?" Leah cried, hugging Josie.
"It's nothing for you to worry about my dear. After all that climbing, you need to get some sleep," Josie replied, trying to soothe her daughter.

She tucked Leah in and told her how much she loved her.

"Mummy, can you please read me a bedtime story?"
"Okay, but it is going to have to be a short one," Josie smiled as she picked a book from the pile beside her daughter's bed.

Josie had just about finished a page when she heard a gentle snore. Leah was fast asleep. Josie slowly ran her fingers through her daughter's hair and couldn't help but wonder what would have happened if she had heeded the repugnant advice she was given when pregnant with this bundle of joy.

Just thinking about Leah helped take Josie's mind off Bruce's surprise; it was the perfect distraction. Josie said a prayer and fell asleep almost as soon as her head hit the pillow.

15
Bruce's Surprise

After the thunderstorm from the night before, seeing the sun shine so brightly was a welcome sight to behold. Today was all about the anticipated arrival of Bruce and his guest, but as his flight was scheduled to land just before noon, they all had a well-deserved lie-in. Well, apart from Angela.

Angela had woken up at the crack of dawn to prepare the spare room for her son. Once she finished cleaning it, she woke Josie up to help lay fresh linen on the bed and add a few other finishing touches while she went to the kitchen to make breakfast.

Josie had made up her mind to act as if she knew nothing, as if she never heard her parent's conversation, as if she didn't know what her brother was up to. So, when her mum told her to sort out Bruce's room, she pretended to do it with a spring in her step and an exaggerated smile that almost made her face ache.

At precisely two minutes past three that afternoon, a taxi pulled up in front of the villa, and when the driver blew the horn, everyone ran out to see Bruce. Everyone except Josie, who wasn't looking forward to meeting her brother's surprise guest. She could hear Daphne and Lois screaming excitedly and then arguing over who was going to roll his suitcase inside.

"So Bruce, I heard you have a surprise for us. Where is she?" Angela asked, trying to sound as normal as possible.
"Oh, I dropped her off at her friend's place, but she's coming for dinner tomorrow if that's okay?"
"But your father said…"

Angela felt her husband's arm nudge her lightly, and then she saw Josie walking towards them. Josie noticed the nudge but played along. To her surprise, Bruce was alone. "Maybe he changed his mind," she thought.

"Hi Bruce," Josie smiled as she gave her brother a big hug.
"How was your flight?"
"The flight was good. I actually slept through most of it. Wow, this place is lovely!"
"It sure is. Wait till you see the garden."
"If you slept through the flight, then you must be hungry," Angela butted in.
"I am," Bruce replied.

Daphne and Lois had hurriedly dropped their brother's suitcase in his room, and along with Emily and Leah, started bombarding Bruce with all sorts of questions.

"Alright ladies, first let me grab something to eat and catch a few winks, then I promise to fill you in on what I have been up to. Is that okay?"
"Okay," the girls chorused.

With Carol busy ironing in the utility room and the girls playing in the garden, Josie suspected that her mum had used food to lure Bruce into the kitchen so she could have a word with him alone. So, even though she was tempted, Josie joined her dad in the living room.

John looked surprised as he had assumed she would help her mum in the kitchen, but instead of saying anything, he just smiled.

"You know what, dad, I think I should write a book about my life experiences and future expectations. What do you think?"

"I remember you mentioned that before, but then you also said that you desired to open a home for sexually abused girls. Are you still thinking of going ahead with that?"

"Yes, I am. That is my number one priority, and plans are quietly in motion. I can assure you that it is the one thing I will never give up on."

"So, what have you done so far? You do know that whenever you are ready, our firm can help out when it comes to registering your company?"

"Thank you, dad. I was actually going to ask you about that. I believe once that is up and running, everything else will fall into place. I am also making enquiries about setting one up in Nigeria too."

"Really!" John exclaimed. "Have you taken into consideration the laws of that land, and who will run it when you are not there?"

"Don't worry about that dad, I have quite a few friends over there, and besides, I know I can count on Bosede and her family to help out. By the way, did I tell you that Bosede and her fiancé are coming to London next week for a short holiday?"

"I thought you said her older sister was getting married?" John looked puzzled.

"Yes, she is, but that is in the States. Her traditional wedding is coming up next month in Lagos, remember?"

She suddenly noticed that her dad was looking at her funny, and then he started laughing, almost choking in the process. "Dad, what's the matter, why are you looking at me like that?" a perplexed Josie asked.

The special moment shared between Josie and her father was interrupted when her mother, followed by her brother, walked into the room and promptly sat down. Bruce looked at his mother, and she gave her son the nod.

"So, the moment has finally come," Josie thought.

She knew that her mum must have persuaded her brother to come clean. So, showing no emotion, she waited for him to speak, prepared to give him the benefit of the doubt.

Bruce cleared his throat.

"What I am about to say may not go down well, especially with you Josie, but please hear me out."

It dawned on Josie that her brother, who was never lost for words, was struggling, and for some strange reason which she could not understand, she wanted him to stop. But it was too late, there was no going back now. She looked him straight in the eye and waited with bated breath.

"I flew in with Peggy Jones, your former classmate at St Magdalene's College. We actually started seeing each other after she gave evidence against you. My plan then was to discredit her and show everyone that she was a gold digger, one who couldn't be trusted…"
"So, what happened?" Josie interrupted, squirming in her seat.
"Josie, Peggy confessed to me that the Dolands paid her to testify against you, but she did not do it for the money.

Apparently, she has always envied you, your achievements, and how everyone seemed to like and speak well of you. Her aim was simply to ruin your reputation."

"So, what happened? Why are you still seeing her?" Josie was seething. She felt she was going to erupt, but somehow she managed to contain herself.

"Well, like I said, it all started because I had an ulterior motive, but over time I began to see another side to her. The more we spoke, the more I realised how much Peggy regretted what she had done and how she wanted to make amends. So, out of her own volition, Peggy visited Lady Donna. She told her she was withdrawing her statement and tried to return the money. However, on the advice of her lawyer, Lady Donna refused and instead threatened to deal with Peggy if she did not testify against you as agreed. So, even though I encouraged her to retract her statement, Peggy was the one who decided to tell the police everything that happened, and she also handed the money over to them."

"But the harm has already been done," Josie declared. "Right now, she is the last person I want to see. I'm sorry."

"Josie, I totally understand how you feel. All I am saying is that you hear her out. Give her a chance to tell you her side of the story. The sole reason why she made the trip with me was to apologise to you personally and ask for your forgiveness."

"Yeah, that's rather convenient. Are you sure you're not doing this for the sake of your relationship because from what I can see, Peggy has got you wrapped around her finger?"

"So, what did the police tell Peggy after she withdrew her statement because I don't remember you telling me this part of the story?" Angela asked impatiently.

"The police were obviously not happy with her for wasting their time, but advised that she would have to come back in when they start sorting out the evidence."

"Well, Josie, the decision is yours to make, but I think you should listen to what Peggy has to say," John said, looking appealingly at his daughter.

By nature, Josie was not a cantankerous person, and she usually tried to steer clear of anything that could bring about a disagreement. But now everyone was trying to appeal to her good nature, asking her to forgive a girl who has never liked her. What she couldn't understand was, even though she and Peggy were in the same ancient history club at school, they were never friends.

She loved her family and appreciated what Bruce had done by confronting someone who lied against her, going to the extreme extent of befriending her to prove that the girl was a liar. Honestly, she couldn't understand how her brother ended up liking Peggy, but it seemed her case was one of someone who was lost but now found, blind but now could see.

Josie turned to her parents.

"Bruce should have discussed this with me in advance to at least know how I would feel, but now that she is here purportedly to make peace, I will go with whatever decision you make. However, I will not speak with her alone. My one condition is that Peggy will say whatever she has to say in front of everyone, including Mrs Pearce and the girls. That way, she will have to think twice before lying again."

"Well, son, I guess tomorrow after dinner it is then," John said.

Bruce looked a bit reluctant, but if that was the price that had to be paid, he was ready to go ahead with it. He just wondered how Peggy would feel apologising in front of everyone.

16
Padre Domingo

Their time on the island went by so quickly. The owners of the villa usually had cleaners come to the house once their guests had left, but on the eve of their departure, Angela and Carol got everyone to chip in with the cleaning in one way or another. Carol was especially keen on making sure that Daphne, Lois, Emily, and Leah were involved as it would help them learn how to be good housekeepers and not wait for others to clean up after them.

That afternoon, Josie decided to visit the Iglesia de Santo Domingo de Guzmán, an ancient church known for its sixteen-century frescoes and adornments. She told her brother she wanted to do some last-minute sightseeing, but really Josie needed some time alone to reflect on her recent encounter with Peggy Jones. Everyone else seemed to accept what her former schoolmate had said. Even Mrs Pearce, who could be sceptical at times, seemed swayed, but Josie had her doubts. According to Josie, there was just something about her story. It was too contrived, too smooth.

As Josie examined the frescoes, she noticed a priest walking towards her. The last thing she needed right now was someone interrupting her thought pattern. She turned and tried to melt into the crowd, but it was too late. Josie felt a gentle touch on her shoulder. She turned and looked up at the tall, elderly man in a black frock, his eyes were so soft and kind. Then to her surprise, the old man introduced himself in English with an American accent.

"Hello, I am Father Dominic, but everyone here calls me Padre Domingo."
"Hello Padre Domingo, are you American?" Josie stuttered nervously. "Oh, I am so sorry, please forgive me. My name is Josephine. I am here on holiday with my family."
"I knew from the moment I saw you enter the church that you were a tourist. Well, in answer to your question, yes, I am originally from America. I was born in Milwaukee sixty-five years ago, but I have only been back a couple times since I arrived here."
"Oh, really," Josie exclaimed.

Father Dominic's gaze left Josie momentarily as he noticed a couple of young people enter the church nave.

"Sorry, could you give me a second, please?"

The padre briefly excused himself and went over to talk to the young visitors only to find out that they were part of a larger group of tourists. So he ushered one of the young intern priests over to show the group around before making his way back to Josie who was still taking in the linings and the pictures on the wall.

"I can see that you are drawn to the paintings."
"Well, I have always been a fan of paintings, historical artefacts, and ancient buildings. They have a certain je ne sais quoi about them," Josie replied.
"I agree with you. It is one of the reasons why we do not allow tourists to take photographs inside the building. Then

of course, there is also the issue of security. Sadly, we have suffered several burglaries in the past and to curb this we recently installed CCTV security cameras both inside and outside the building that record everything, twenty-four hours a day, seven days a week."

"So, since installing these preventive measures, have you had any security issues?" Josie asked curiously.

"Oh, yes. Remember, we are dealing with human beings, and I can assure you that we have had our fair share of attempted robberies," Father Dominic smiled.

"Wow!" Josie exclaimed.

"So, tell me, what is on your mind?"

Josie could see the sympathetic look in the padre's eyes as he looked at her.

"Nothing," Josie countered.

Unfortunately, the flash of anger in her response gave her away.

"My dear, from the moment you entered the building, I could see uncertainty and bemusement written all over your face, as if you were running away from something. I know I am an old man, but I just might be able to help if the good Lord gives me the wisdom and grace to do so."

The padre kept his kind gaze on her as he waited for a response. Josie plonked herself down in a nearby seat, put her face in her hands, and sobbed silently. The old man sat beside her quietly and waited patiently. When she eventually sat up, the priest offered Josie his handkerchief.

Josie wiped her tears, and as she handed the handkerchief back, she could see from the look in the old man's eyes that he was still waiting for an answer. She folded her hands on her lap, looked at him and smiled tentatively.

"Thank you for being so kind." Josie hesitated, then continued. "You are right, I do have a lot on my mind, but I am not running away from anything. I am just trying to figure out why those I trust always seem to think that they know what's best for me and interfere in situations that don't concern them. Why won't they just leave me alone and let me handle things my way? Or am I being unreasonable?"

"Well, I guess it depends on the situation. I know beyond a shadow of a doubt that you came here today for a reason."

"And what might that be?" Josie retorted.

"To find peace, and I believe I just might be able to help," the old man answered.

Josie, not knowing what came over her, began to blurt out her whole life history to this stranger, including things she hadn't divulged to anyone except the Archibongs. She was weeping by the time she finished telling her story, and so the priest was left with no other option than to cradle her in his arms. Strangely enough, Josie felt a warm, peaceful feeling slowly flow through her. When she finally stopped crying, she looked at her watch and let out a scream which startled Father Dominic.

"What is the matter?" he asked

"I need to get back to the villa as soon as possible. My family will be worried stiff."

She jumped up and was about to make her way out when she felt the priest gently hold her back.

"Please sit down and listen to me for a second. I have been in this business for almost thirty years, so trust me, I know a thing or two. You see, my father was a farmer who ran a very successful farming business, and as I was the first of three children, he naturally expected that I would take over once he died. So, imagine how shocked he was when I told him that I was going to be a priest."

Josie noticed the nostalgic look on his face.

"Before I knew what was happening, my father had called a family meeting which, apart from my mother and my siblings, also included his brothers and sisters. Here's what he told me: "Listen to me, Dominic Milder, or maybe I should call you Pope Domingo the sixth. As you have decided not to take on the responsibility of looking after the Milder farming business, which has been passed down over many generations, and insisted on this damn priesthood thing, I put it to you today with my entire family as witnesses, that you will be a wretched man, a beggar for life. And don't you ever come back and ask me for a dime because from today onwards you are no longer my son. You are dead to me!""

"No, surely your dad would never say that!" Josie exclaimed, aghast at what she just heard.

"Oh yes, he did," Father Dominic winked. "The day after that meeting, I packed my possessions and left. I can still see my mother's tears and hear the cries of my siblings. I almost changed my mind, but I was so sure that I was meant to be a priest."

The old man told his captive audience how he immediately went to their bishop to make his intentions known. He was almost twenty-one at the time, so he didn't need parental consent. The Bishop called the Sacred Heart Seminary and School of Theology, and after a brief interview with the Principal, he was admitted. In his final year, the school was asked to recommend some enthusiastic seminarians for priesthood internships overseas, and when the opportunity was offered to him, he jumped at it. After all, he no longer had a home to return to.

Father Dominic told Josie how his mother, who was an artist, would visit him secretly under the pretext that she was going for one art exhibition or the other.

The padre's story was going on a bit longer than she thought it would. She needed to get back to the villa, but at the same time, Josie wanted to hear the end of the story. The old man noticed Josie twitching her fingers anxiously.

"Sorry for keeping you, my dear. Let me cut the story short, and don't worry about getting back home. I will drive you back myself. It is not that far away from here, anyway."

Father Dominic continued his story.

"So, that is how twelve other freshers and I landed on these shores. Remember, I said I have only been back to the States a few times since my arrival here? Well, each time was to attend the funeral of a loved one. First, it was my father who died of a heart attack, then my mother's brother and then my dad's youngest brother."

"Did you reconcile with your father before he died?" Josie asked, still engrossed in the old man's story.

"Oh, yes, I did. My mother called one night and asked if I had enough to buy a ticket home. I remember asking her why, and that is when she told me that my father was dying and I needed to see him. I knew my dad didn't want to see me and that the request to come home was my mother's idea, but I agreed anyway, " the old man reminisced. "Anyway, I think it's about time I took you home," Father Dominic said, rising to his feet.

He asked Josie to wait for him while he brought his car round to the front of the building.

As the padre walked away, Josie fell to her knees and said a short prayer before standing up and making her way to the front door.

Walking out of the building, she noticed a brand new Chevrolet coming round the corner. To her utmost surprise, the old priest was driving it.

Father Dominic couldn't help but laugh when he saw the look of awe on Josie's face. He pulled up, jumped out, and opened the door for her to enter. As the padre drove her home, Josie still found it hard to understand why this not so bad looking old man with a sturdy, muscular physique ended up being a priest. Okay, she knew he was convinced that he was meant to be one, but she could just imagine how a younger version of him could be anything he wanted to be.

"You're still wondering why I chose to be a priest when I could so easily have been a Hollywood film star, aren't you?" It was as if he had read her mind. "Well, my younger brother chose that path, and when he became famous, he changed his name to Stanley Wysel, also known as the Hollywood stuntman. I am sure you must have watched some of his movies. His daring stunts almost gave our mother a heart attack," he chuckled.

As the priest manoeuvred through the narrow cobbled streets, Josie remembered the question she wanted to ask him.

"So, is your mother still alive?"
"Yes, the old woman is almost eighty-seven, but still alive and kicking. She has had her ups and downs healthwise, but she's going strong. In fact, she still paints and attends art exhibitions, and as if that's not enough, she also runs the family business alongside my younger sister and her husband."
At that point, they pulled up in front of the villa.
"Father Dominic, thank you so much for everything."
"You're welcome, Josie. By the way, listen to your parents on this one. I get the feeling that the Peggy girl is telling the

truth and with her testimony, there is a good chance you can turn the tables on the Dolands and get the justice you so earnestly desire."

Josie opened the door, and as she was about to step out of the car, she invited the priest to meet the rest of the family, but he declined.

"My dear, I shall be praying for you. This year I intend to retire and move back to America. I want to be with my aged mother when she finally decides to pass on. After everything she has done for me, it is the least I can do."
"Well, I wish you all the best Padre Domingo," Josie said. "And I will try not to disappoint you."
"God bless you, my daughter. Go in peace." The priest smiled as he drove away.

Josie had spent well over four hours in the church, and she knew that once she entered the villa, everyone would want to know what kept her so long. So, when she walked through the front door and saw all the anxious faces, she began to laugh.

"Okay guys, relax, I only went to the Iglesia de Santo Domingo de Guzmán to take a look at the famous paintings and frescoes, and I did tell Bruce before I left. Where is he anyway?"
"Well, it wasn't that easy to stay calm, especially as no one seemed to know your whereabouts," her mum replied angrily. "Anyway, your brother went to see Peggy."
"I am sorry if I gave you all a scare. I didn't mean to. Anyway, regarding the Peggy situation, after giving it some thought, I believe she is telling the truth and honestly wants to help. So, all is well."

With that, they all rushed over and gave her a big hug.

17
Concerns

The flight back to England was a turbulent one, but they landed safely at about five o'clock on Monday evening. After clearing Customs Control, they hopped on the bus which took them from the terminal to the Long Stay car park where John and Bruce parked their cars.

They all said their goodbyes, with Josie struggling to hold back her tears as she hugged her daughter, then Angela, Daphne, Lois and Josie piled into their car, while Carol, Emily, Leah and Peggy got into Bruce's.

The Kimberley's were all tired when they finally got home, and while Angela, Josie and the girls went straight upstairs to freshen up, John was left to carry all the luggage inside before making himself a cup of coffee.

When Bruce got to Mrs Pearce's place, both Emily and Leah were sound asleep. So, Peggy helped Carol take the girls inside while Bruce brought in the suitcases. The drive to Peggy's place in Hendon was an uncomfortably quiet one. They both knew beforehand that their plan to go to Tenerife would have consequences, but Peggy still wasn't sure if she had convinced Josie.

Just as Bruce was about to open the car door for Peggy, she looked up at him.

"Do you think Josie has really forgiven me?" She asked, her voice trembling. "I mean, I know we hugged each other and all that, but it seemed like she only accepted my apology because you were all there. It was almost as if she didn't want to create a scene."

"Peggy, I know my sister. She says what's on her mind. If she forgave you, then know that you are forgiven. Just give her time," Bruce said, holding her hand reassuringly.

"Alright, if you say so, Bruce."

Bruce walked Peggy to her front door before waving goodbye and promising to call her the following day. Driving back to his parent's place, his phone, which was in his pocket, began to vibrate. From the car display screen, he saw it was his mum.

"Hello mum, is everything okay?" he asked.

"Sorry to be a bother, but could you please get us something to eat from Spicy Basil. We're all tired, and the last thing I want to do is cook."

"No problem, mum. See you soon."

So, Bruce called the restaurant and placed his order in the hope that it would be ready by the time he got there.

Mindful that he had some very hungry mouths waiting for him, once he picked up his order, Bruce drove home as fast as he could. When he walked through the front door, the atmosphere was calm, and though they were all hungry, everyone looked happy. Bruce found it hard to believe that the family had managed to make it back from Tenerife in one piece considering the bombshell he had dropped on them, but as they all sat down to eat, he felt a warmness flow through him. It had been a while, but it felt good to be home.

After they had finished eating, and Daphne and Lois had gone to bed, John decided to bring up the elephant in the room, the Doland case.

"I guess we all know that this matter is in the hands of the Crown Prosecutors," he said.

"But we also have our own lawyer keeping tabs on things," Josie added. "By the way, I have done some research myself, and you will be shocked to know the number of cases decided as far back as the fifties by the then House of Lords that are still relevant today. I came across outstanding pronouncements on sexual offence cases made by the Lord Cross of Chelsea, and the former Master of the Rolls, Lord Justice Denning also gets my vote. They did not beat about the bush when delivering judgment."

"Maybe you should have studied Law instead of International Relations," her dad chuckled.

"Dad, I am being serious," Josie said, throwing her father a chastening look. "Looking at the provisions of The Sexual Offences Act 2003, the maximum penalty for raping a child under the age of thirteen is life imprisonment. And in my case, he is going to have to prove mutual consent. So personally, I am feeling quite confident."

"We are not thinking of allowing Leah to give evidence in an open court, are we?" Angela asked.

"Of course not," Josie declared.

Angela heaved a sigh of relief.

"I just hope there will be no reporting restrictions on the

case," Josie continued. "I recently read about the Huddersfield grooming, where twenty men have been found guilty. As one of the reporters put it, 'The sexual abuse of vulnerable children in English towns is dominating our news and overwhelming our police and our courts. It is a crime that, until recently, was rarely discussed in public. Child sexual abuse was often ignored or covered up, and the protection of the institutional reputation or community cohesion put before the protection of children.' Can you beat that? What is it with men and rape? I honestly do not understand!" Josie was visibly frustrated.

"Calm down, my dear. I am sure the Commissioner of Police and the Crown Prosecution are well prepared for this case," John assured his daughter.

While they discussed the upcoming case, Bruce put on the television, and suddenly their attention was drawn to a crowd of reporters standing on the stairs of what looked like a police station, questioning a distinguished-looking, grey-haired gentleman.

"Mr Quinn, I am sure you are aware that if your client is found guilty, he will be in the cooler for a considerable length of time?"

"Well, I am sure you have heard the phrase, 'Innocent until proven guilty'? My client is from one of the most influential families in the land, and when people make accusations that can easily be refuted, they lay themselves out for ridicule. To the best of my knowledge, my client is innocent, and I intend to prove it."

"But the evidence is stacked up against your client. Surely there is no way you can prove his innocence."

"My track record speaks for itself. There is a reason why I hardly ever lose a case, and I do not expect this one to be any different. I have nothing more to say. Thank you."

"But Mr Quinn…" a persistent reporter began, but it was

too late. The gentleman turned and walked straight into the building, ensuring there was no further altercation between him and the horde of photographers and reporters.

"Wow, he's rather cocky!" Josie exclaimed.

"Well, that is Mr Quinn for you," John replied. "They say he is one of the top barristers in the land and is known for his brutal cross-examination techniques in court. He specialises in getting men who have been accused of rape off the hook by bullying the victims."

"And the judge actually allows that?" Bruce asked, looking a bit confused. "I thought that lawyers who did that were usually reprimanded by the judge. So, how does he get away with it?"

"Maybe they feel intimidated by him," Josie said, expressing her resentment. "If other lawyers and maybe even the Crown Prosecutors feel threatened by this man, then what chance does the rape victim have?"

"It is not all about intimidation, my daughter," John shook his head. "I know it sounds strange, but you would be surprised at how many of these top legal luminaries belong to the same secret societies. So like it or not, they tend to look out for each other."

John's phone rang. It was the Kimberleys legal representative, Mr Salmon Goldberg, and he sounded concerned. He asked if they had seen Mr Quinn on television and wanted to know what their thoughts were.

"We're fine," John replied. "We were expecting the usual braggadocio, but we're not moved. Mr Quinn will soon realise that he has met his match. We are ready to fight to the bitter end."

"That is precisely what I wanted to hear. Also, I thought you would like to know that the suspect is going to be arraigned before the Magistrate court next week before the case is transferred to the Old Bailey. Hopefully, the hearing should commence within three weeks from now."

"Okay Sal, please don't hesitate to call me if there are any new developments, and thank you for believing in us."

John dropped the phone and turned to tell the rest of the family what their lawyer had said. By the time he finished, it was almost eleven o'clock. So, they all said their goodnights and went to bed.

Angela was a bit worried about her daughter; after everything that had happened that evening, she wasn't sure if Josie would get any sleep. However, on the contrary, not only did her daughter fall asleep the second she hit her bed, but she was also the last to wake up the next morning.

Going by the way Josie went about the day humming cheerfully, she seemed not to have a care in the world. But, deep down inside her priorities hadn't changed; she wanted Leah back and Michael Doland behind bars.

Angela made sure she kept a watchful eye on her daughter. There was something strange about the way she was behaving, especially with the court case looming. But as long as her daughter was happy then so was she.

18
The Trial

Exactly three weeks from the day Mr Quinn made his pronouncements, the members of the jury, who had been chosen during the preceding week, filed into the Old Bailey Court to commence the hearing of the case; R vs Michael Doland.

When the case was called, all the accused was required to do was confirm his name and address, after which the case was adjourned to Friday, allowing time for both parties to prepare their respective witnesses.

That Friday, the trial resumed inside Court 12 of the Old Bailey, and the nervous excitement in the atmosphere was tangible. At last, the long-awaited trial was finally here.

The presiding judge, Mr Declan Horace, was known for his impatience with dithering counsels who had no respect for the bench, and he often exhibited his anger during hearings. But he was also a fair and keen observer. As he made his entrance, everyone in the courtroom was told to stand.

Once the Judge was seated, the court clerk asked the defendant, Michael Doland and his barrister if they were ready to proceed with the trial to which the defending counsel nodded and replied with an air of familiarity that bordered on frivolity. This behaviour was duly noted by a female member of the jury, a teacher by profession, who as a result, took an instant dislike to both the defendant and his counsel. She, however, managed to keep a straight face, not giving her feelings away.

The judge then asked both the Prosecutor and counsel for the defence to approach the bench.

"Gentlemen," Judge Horace began. "I just want to warn you that I will not tolerate any theatrical antics in my court. Do you understand?
"Yes, my lord," they both chorused, and with that, they returned to their seats.

Then the judge asked the court clerk to read out the charges against the defendant.

"In the case of aggravated rape of a minor in his care, the defendant has been charged with the following: Ten Counts of rape, ten counts of False Imprisonment, four counts of Sexual Assault, three counts of Breach of Trust and five counts of Incest."

After the charges had been heard, Judge Horace addressed the jury panel, which was made up of six men and six women.

"The defendant is Michael Doland. He is an accountant by profession, and he has previously worked in a public school as a supply teacher. During the course of this trial, we will play a recording of the victim's testimony. For clarification purposes, the victim will be identified as 'Child A'."

Having laid out the preambles, the judge invited both parties to give their opening statements. This was duly carried out, with the prosecution declaring that they intended to prove beyond any reasonable doubt the guilt of the accused, while the defence told the jury that their intention was to prove that their client had no case to answer. After that, the prosecuting barrister rose to his feet and called his first witness.

"Can you please state your name and occupation."
"My name is Caroline Pearce. I am an independent cosmetics consultant representative."
"Can you tell the court how you got to know the victim."
"One morning, my daughter and I were at Highbury and Islington station, on our way to Birmingham when we happened to see the victim, Child A. She was huddled up in a corner on a bench shivering. She looked sick and…"
"Objection, my lord. The witness has no medical experience and therefore has no business talking about the victim's state of health."
"Sustained. Mrs Pearce could you tell the court what happened next."

After the prosecutor had led Mrs Pearce in evidence without any further interruptions from the defending counsel, he called his next witness, Inspector Gerald, the Police officer who attended to Leah after Mrs Pearce found her.

Inspector Gerald told the court how he met Child A, and how, after interviewing her and learning that she had been abused, he instructed his men to take her to the hospital immediately. He also informed the court that as the victim was a child and had refused to tell him who her parents were, he had arranged a press conference in the hope that someone would be able to identify her.

Witness after witness was called to the stand among which were the doctors and nurses who attended to Leah when she was admitted to the hospital and the social worker who was with her during the police interview. Then out of nowhere, the prosecutor called Mrs Elsie Doland, the wife of the accused, to take the stand. Immediately the counsel for the defence sprang to his feet.

"Objection, objection," he shouted. "The defence was not informed that the defendant's spouse would be called as a prosecuting witness. A wife cannot give evidence against her husband."

The judge turned to the prosecuting barrister.

"My lord, according to R v Lapworth (1930), a spouse can be compelled to witness against a spouse for the prosecution as this relates to rape and personal violence," the prosecutor alleged. "Also, Section 80 of the Police and Criminal Evidence Act 1984 restores the ability of the prosecution to compel the testimony of the spouse of the accused where the defendant has been charged with "assault on, or injury or a threat of injury to" the spouse or a child under 16, or a sexual offence toward a child under 16."

There was some rabble-rousing in the public gallery, which prompted the judge to call for order. When the courtroom was finally quiet, Judge Horace threatened to have anyone who tried to disrupt the trial escorted out by the security guards. He then asked both counsels to approach the bench.

"Gentlemen, I told you before we started that this court will not tolerate any indiscipline from any of you. If there is anything to discuss as a matter of law, we will look into it together. However, I would have expected the defending counsel to know about the provisions of Section 80 of the Police and Criminal Evidence Act 1984, as well as the subsequent enactment of Section 53 of the Youth Justice and

Criminal Evidence Act 1999."

After admonishing them, the judge adjourned the case until the following Monday. The court clerk asked everyone to stand while Judge Horace rose from his seat and left the courtroom still smarting at the lack of respect exhibited by both counsels.

As Michael Doland was escorted out by the guards, his mother gave him a hug and assured him that the case would collapse and ultimately be dismissed, and if the worst came to the worst, his jail sentence would be mitigated considering their status in the society.

19
Harassed

O n their way out of the court building, the Kimberleys ran into Michael Doland's children, Michael Jr and Dora May, and his two older sisters, Winifred and Jennifer. It felt a bit strange that they were all on the same side, considering they were related to Michael Doland, but Michael's sisters had decided to stand for the truth. They knew their brother was guilty of a grave crime, and if going to jail was the price he had to pay, then so be it.

While the grown-ups were talking, Michael Jr and Dora May gently pulled Leah to one side and gave her a warm hug.

"Leah, we are so sorry you have to go through this torture. Just remember that you will always be our sister, and we are here whenever you need us. We love you so much," Dora May said, struggling to hold back the tears.

"It's not your fault. You guys have always been there for me, and I love you too. I just hope it all ends soon."

"Not to worry, it will soon be over, and more importantly, my dad will be in a place where he can never hurt you or anyone else again. I just hate him so much right now, and I hope he rots in jail," Michael Jr declared passionately, a deadly look in his eyes.

"Michael, calm down! Now is not the time for all that." Dora May said, giving her brother a stern look.

"But, you feel the same way too, Dora." Michael quietly hit back at his sister.

"That's not the point, Michael. Like I said, now is not the time for all that," Dora May reiterated.

"Okay guys, we all need to relax," Leah said with a calm smile. "I know this is tough for all of us, but my mum said it's all going to be fine in the end, and I believe her."

Just about then, Dora May spotted their mum and grandma Bertha waving, indicating that it was time to go home. They both said goodbye to Leah and promised to see her on Monday.

Afterwards, Leah ran over to where the Kimberleys and Carol Pearce were standing. Winifred and Jennifer had already left, and now they were talking to the Commissioner of Police, Mr Dominic Parkes who advised them to stay focussed and to prepare for what he called the Quinn backlash. Mr Parkes knew that come Monday, the defence would try all they could to intimidate and discredit every witness called by the prosecution. He also told Josie to stay calm when she takes the witness stand because Mr Quinn will definitely try to get under her skin.

"I suppose your lawyer would have briefed you anyway," the Commissioner concluded, and right then, Mr Goldberg, their lawyer, walked up behind them.

As Mr Parkes took his leave, Mr Goldberg, the Kimberleys, Carol, Emily and Leah went to grab some lunch in a nearby restaurant, but when they got there, they all seemed to lose their appetite. All the same, they ordered some nibbles, and when the waiter placed the food in front of them, they picked at it nonchalantly. They obviously wanted to talk about what they had just witnessed in court, but for some reason, there was a reluctance to broach the topic. Then Bruce's phone rang. It was Peggy. He excused himself and stepped outside the restaurant.

"Hi Bruce, where are you?"
"We are at a restaurant near the court building, but I think we'll be leaving soon. Why, what's the matter?"
"Oh, nothing really. It's just that now the case has actually started, I'm a bit scared."
"There's no need to be scared. After all, you told Lady Donna's lawyer that you will not be testifying against Josie, or have you changed your mind again?" Bruce asked brusquely.
"Of course not. I am just afraid of what Michael's mother might do."
"Come on Peggy, don't let that woman get into your head. I know it's not easy, but I believe in you. We all know that when you take the stand, the defence will try and discredit you as a witness, but if you stay calm and stick to the truth, you have nothing to worry about."

There was more to her call, but she couldn't tell him over the phone.

"Okay Bruce, I will talk to you later," Peggy whispered.

Bruce didn't like the vibes he was getting from his girlfriend, and he wondered why she would be in two minds about helping his sister. Something must have happened, and he was determined to find out. He needed to see Peggy as soon as possible.

He somehow managed to find a way to leave the restaurant without too many questions being asked, and making the assumption that Peggy would be home, he jumped on the next train to Hendon.

When he arrived in Hendon, Bruce phoned Peggy. Luckily, even though she wasn't home, she was nearby. So, he asked if she could meet him in the Costa Coffee shop near the station.

Bruce ordered a caramel cortado and was about to sit down when Peggy walked in. She spotted him and made her way to the table. Bruce gave her a hug, and they both sat down.

"Wow, that was quick," Bruce said.
"Well, I was actually in the repair shop around the corner. I came to pick up my iPad," Peggy replied.

Bruce asked if she wanted something to drink, but she declined briskly. He noticed that she was looking a bit nervous and trying to avoid eye contact. So, he took her hands and gently squeezed them assuredly.

"Peggy, look at me. Why are you so jittery? What is the matter?"
"I'm sorry, Bruce."
"Peggy, what aren't you telling me?"

Stuttering and looking over her shoulder as if someone was after her, she told him what had happened. Peggy knew that being in this situation was all her fault, but despite making it explicitly clear that she no longer wanted anything to do with them, it was beginning to look like she would have no choice but to yield to Lady Donna's request. However, what was causing Peggy the most trepidation was that thanks to Michael's mother, her mum and dad had caught wind of what she had gotten herself into. The heartless woman had tracked down her parents and told them that their daughter was blackmailing her son.

"Bruce, that woman told my parents that I had asked for money and that when they refused to pay me, I went to the police to give a false statement that incriminated her son. Can you imagine that!" Peggy was trembling all over.

She told Bruce how she had been confronted by her parents. Her father, who was generally a mild-mannered, laid back gentleman, had told her in no uncertain terms how disappointed he was, and who could blame him? He had instilled discipline and dignity in all of his children, and he expected better. Her mum couldn't believe why her daughter would blackmail someone for money. After all, it wasn't as if they were poor.

"Don't you understand what could happen if the police found out? What were you thinking?" her mother screamed. She was furious.

Peggy told Bruce how she had waited for her parents to finish dressing her down before telling them her side of the story.

"So, what did you do with it?" her mum asked after she mentioned that Lady Donna had offered her money in exchange for her fake testimony.

"Mum, are you listening to me? I said that I tried to return the money, but the woman refused to take it back. That is when I reported myself to the police and handed the money to them."

"Well, after explaining everything to my parents, I still don't think they believed me, and when mum called me a disgrace, I just couldn't take it anymore. That's when I ran out of the room and called you."

"I believe you Peggy and I want you to know that you did the right thing. If you hadn't handed that money over to the police, I can assure you that Lady Donna would somehow use it against you. That's what she does, she is an evil woman!"

"But Bruce, don't you see?" Peggy said, her eyes filling with tears. "It will be my word against theirs, and since I have no witnesses to corroborate the bribe offer, where will that leave me?"

"Calm down, Peggy. Are you sure you don't want me to get you something to drink?" Bruce asked.

"I am fine and thank you for listening. I actually feel a lot better now that I've managed to get the damn thing off my chest. Anyway, enough about me. How did the hearing go?"

"Actually, everything was going pretty well until Michael's wife was called to the witness stand and the defence objected vehemently!"

"Why?"

"Apparently he objected to the defendant's wife giving evidence against her husband."

"Oh, wow! So, what happened next?"

"Well, both counsels turned the courtroom into a verbal boxing ring and had to be called to order by the judge. He told them to approach the bench to consult on what he termed, 'a matter of law'. After that, he publicly admonished both parties and told them to use the weekend to put their cases in order as he would not tolerate such unruly indiscipline in his court again. Then he adjourned the case till Monday."

"Did he really say that to them?"

"He sure did. In fact, if it wasn't for the seriousness of the case, what happened today could easily have been called a comedy of errors," Bruce laughed, and so did Peggy. Her nerves seemed to have disappeared.

"By the way, how is your sister taking all this?"

"Josie is a tough cookie, I can tell you that!" Bruce replied. "Sometimes, I just don't know what's on her mind. The Josie I used to know is so different from the new Josie."

"And why do you say that?"

Bruce looked on quietly, a bemused expression on his face. Peggy coughed.

"Oh, I am so sorry. What did you say?"

"Never mind. I understand if you do not want to talk about it. It's not that important anyway."

"Well, Josie is fine. She is taking each day one step at a time. The girl is a fighter."

"Oh my God, Bruce, look at the time," Peggy said glancing

at the clock on the café wall. "I need to get back home before my parents have another go at me."

"Maybe it's time to start thinking about getting a place of your own."

"I totally agree with you. It is one thing I am strongly considering at the moment."

"Well, on second thought, maybe you should exercise a bit of patience, especially with the Lady Donna breathing down your neck."

Bruce walked Peggy home and waited until she had closed the front door before he left. He was in a better mood as he jumped on the train home. Peggy had promised him that if the defence asked her to take the stand, she would not give evidence against Josie even if it made her a hostile witness.

20

The Picnic

I t was a bright sunny Saturday morning, and as Josie rolled out of bed, she smiled, remembering what had happened in the courtroom the day before. Today, however, was all about her and Leah. Josie had looked forward to this day since that moment in Tenerife when Carol had graciously agreed that she could spend the day with her daughter.

Josie planned to take Leah to Hampstead Heath so they could spend some quality mother and daughter time together. Where initially, she was reluctant to meet her daughter, now she simply could not get enough of her. Josie had grown to cherish every little moment spent with Leah, and even though the circumstances through which her little baby girl was brought into the world were not ideal, Josie thanked God for bringing Leah back into her life. Now, more than ever, she was determined to be a loving mother.

Little Leah had been peering out of her window all morning, and as soon as Josie pulled up in front of the house in her small car, she dashed down the stairs, stood by the front door with her rucksack firmly on her back and waited for the bell to ring. And when it did,

Leah flung the door open and flew into Josie's arms.

"Well, someone's excited," Carol smiled warmly.

Leah was beaming with joy.

"Thank you so much for everything," Josie said with a heart full of gratitude.
"You are welcome, Josie. Now hurry along and make sure you have lots of fun."

They both skipped to the car, hand in hand. Josie opened the passenger door, and Leah jumped into the seat and put on her seatbelt.

As she sat behind the wheel, Josie turned to look at Leah and smiled.

"Wow! You look very pretty."
"Thank you, mummy," Leah giggled.
"Well, I hope you slept well because we're going to have a lovely time today," Josie said excitedly.
"Not really. I was too excited thinking about today, but I'm fine," Leah said, still giggling.
"Mummy, where are we going for our picnic?"
"I am taking us somewhere special. A place where we can have lots of fun, and also watch other families enjoy themselves."
"Yippee, I can't wait. Meanwhile, Emily was feeling poorly yesterday."
"Oh, what was the matter with her?" Josie asked.
"I don't know, but she was shivering all over, and her mum was pressing a cold flannel all over her."
"Okay, when we get back, I will pop in and see how she's doing."
"That would be nice," Leah replied.

Leah turned her attention to the scenery as her mother drove until they finally arrived at the Heath.

It was early afternoon, and the place was bursting at the seams. There were picnic revellers everywhere, some spreading their tents while others placed blankets or mats on the grass. The weather was perfect; sunny with a soft, gentle breeze. Josie and Leah found a nice shady patch, spread their mat, and set up a parasol. They brought out their flasks and food containers before comfortably lying down to enjoy the lovely weather. Not too long after, they were both snoozing.

Josie felt something touch her shoulder. Through her tired eyes, she saw a lady in sun shades looking down and smiling at her. With the sun in her eyes, Josie couldn't quite make out who it was. She slowly sat up.

"It's Josie' isn't it?" the lady asked.
"Yes, and who are you?"
"I met you yesterday, remember, outside the Old Bailey. My name is Jennifer, I am Michael Doland's sister."
"Oh, of course. I'm surprised you recognised me considering we only met briefly yesterday?"
"I have been told that I have an excellent memory," Jennifer smiled.

Even though Leah was still lying down, she was wide awake watching her mother and the tall lady she was speaking to. Jennifer noticed that the little girl was no longer sleeping and asked Josie if she could sit down on the mat.

"No problem. It's large enough for the three of us," Josie smiled.

After making herself comfortable, Jennifer looked at Josie.

"Josie, like I said yesterday, we are on the same side. I totally understand if you refuse to have anything to do with my family, but I just want you to know that there is no way I will side with my brother after what he did to you and your daughter."

Josie listened to what Jennifer had to say, but was quite peeved that she had gatecrashed her time with Leah. It dawned on Josie that if she didn't stop the Doland girl, she could end up ruining the whole day, but at the same time, she was not one to be rude to anyone, even if that person was from an obnoxious family like the Dolands. So, she kept listening.

"You may find it hard to believe, but the only person in the Doland family not supporting you is my mother. Even my husband said he would kill my brother if he ever stepped into our house again. I won't bore you with the gory details, but let us just say that my brother is persona non grata."

Josie was beginning to warm up to the lady. "Maybe she really was genuine," she thought.

Out of nowhere, Leah took Jennifer's hand and flashed a big, broad smile.

"I remember you now," Leah said. "You and your daughter used to visit us. I have always wondered why you stopped coming. Even Frances, Dora May and Michael Jr didn't know why."
"My dear, I never wanted to stop visiting, but I had no choice. If I had a hint of suspicion about what was going on, I would have done something about it. It was when I saw your face on the TV and heard that you had run away from home that I knew something was wrong. Please forgive me," Jennifer hugged Leah, tears running down her face.

To Josie's surprise, her daughter hugged Jennifer back. Josie tried to hold back her tears, but she couldn't. It was a dramatic sight; two grown-up women crying in the middle of a park on a warm, sunny day. Interestingly, Josie got the feeling that she and Jennifer could actually be friends.

After getting over the emotions, the two women spoke about the case, and Jennifer assured Josie that her family would stand by the Kimberleys no matter what.

"I know it might sound strange, but when I heard about what happened to Leah, I was in no doubt that my brother was guilty," Jennifer confessed.

Josie had a confession of her own to make.

"I never thought I would see the day when I would actually have a civil conversation with a member of the Doland family. Over the years, I have harboured so much hatred against your family. I blamed all of you for my woes and was determined to get even no matter what or how long it took."
"No one can blame you for that, Josie. I guess I would do exactly the same if I was in your shoes."

Knowing Leah was listening, both of them were very circumspect with their choice of words. There were still so many unanswered questions, but they would have to wait till another day.

"I was going to ask, what are you doing here, anyway?" Josie asked, changing the topic.
"I often come here with my girls. They are actually over by the pond with my husband. He graciously agreed to accompany us today," Jennifer replied.
"What a coincidence!" Josie exclaimed.

Out of nowhere, they heard the rumbling of thunder accompanied by flashes of lightning. People started packing up hurriedly, folding their mats, blankets, and chairs, dismantling their tents and parasols. Then within minutes, the heavens opened up.

"Typical English weather!" Jennifer said, shaking her head.

She said a quick goodbye to Josie and Leah and dashed over to her family.

Josie and Leah gathered all their stuff and ran for the car, which luckily was parked close to the entrance, but that didn't stop them from getting drenched. They sat in the car panting as they dried their hair with a towel and then made fun of how they both ran like maniacs.

"Wow, mummy look at the time. It's almost three o'clock, and we haven't eaten yet. Can we finish our picnic in the car," Leah asked, rubbing her tummy to emphasise that she was hungry.

" Of course, we can. We'll just eat in the car and enjoy the glorious scenery," Josie laughed. "Anyway, we're not going to let a few drops of rain mess up our day, are we?" "No way," Leah chuckled. "As long as we are together, that's good enough for me."

Josie's eyes began to well up with tears, and in a bid to hide them from her daughter, she quickly turned away and got busy bringing out the sandwiches, fruits, some cupcakes and the drinks and laying them all out on the back seat.

"Alright little one, here's the spread, you can pick whatever you want."

Josie smiled as she watched her daughter gobble down her food.

"Wow, we really are hungry," Josie laughed, making fun of

her daughter.

With her mouth full, Leah could only nod her head before pouring herself some orange juice and drinking it in one gulp, almost choking in the process.

"Slow down munchkin, the food isn't running away" Josie smiled as she patted Leah's back. "Are you okay?"
"I am fine, mummy," Leah half-smiled trying to hide her embarrassment.

After they finished eating, they packed up the leftovers and started the drive back to Mrs Pearce's place. The rain had all but stopped. As she drove, Josie began to reminisce on how the day had gone. It wasn't exactly as planned, but it had been a lovely outing all the same. Josie also thought about how beautiful that day would be when she finally won back custody of her daughter.

Leah had already nodded off by the time they pulled up outside the Pearce's front door. Josie gently woke her daughter up, and they both held hands as she rang the doorbell. A smiling Carol opened the door and invited Josie in for a cuppa, to which Josie gladly obliged. Josie was eager to spend as much time with her daughter as she possibly could. She also wanted to find out how Emily was feeling, and she didn't have to wait long.

While Josie and Carol were talking, an excited-looking Emily ran down the stairs and immediately asked Leah how the day went. Josie found herself enjoying the friendly banter between the two girls and was happy that her daughter had found a true friend.

As soon as she finished her cup of tea, Josie got up to leave, and after promising another picnic date, this time with both of the girls, she left for home.

21

Compromised

The weekend quickly went by, and before they knew it, Monday morning was upon them.

Court 12 of the Old Bailey had been cleaned and was ready for the day's trial, and even though it was meant to resume at precisely ten o'clock, members of the public had started queuing for gallery seats as early as eight that morning. It could be adduced that apart from the so-called quasi-celebrity status of the defendant, the main reason for the gripping public interest was the nature of the case.

A father sexually molesting his daughter and therefore committing incest wasn't exactly an everyday occurrence, and even though most of the public had already concluded that the defendant was guilty of this disgraceful, outrageous crime, their opinion meant nothing until proven. Coincidentally, the trial also came at a time when issues of consent and male responsibility were being discussed around dinner tables and in offices, between friends and colleagues everywhere.

As people took their seats in the courtroom, one could sense the nerves. The opposing counsels and their assistants busied themselves with last-minute consultations and sorting out files, while the jurors sat stone-faced, knowing that they had a daunting task ahead of them.

Once again, the court clerk asked everyone to stand as Judge Declan Horace made his entry, and as he took his seat, he told them all to sit. He then declared the court open for the day's trial, and as he looked sternly at the jury, the counsels for the defence and the prosecution, he told the court that he expected the case to be wrapped up within three weeks.

They continued from where they left off on Friday, with the Prosecuting barrister once again calling Mrs Elsie Doland, to take the stand, but in a strange turn of events, Michael's wife denied any knowledge that her husband was sexually abusing Child A.

The counsel knew Elsie was lying because, in Leah's interview with the police, Leah mentioned on several occasions that she reported what happened to Elsie, who she believed to be her mother at the time, but each time she was told to shut up.

"I put it to you that you are lying. You are trying to cover up the part you played in the victim's abuse."
"I don't know what you are talking about," Elsie responded

The defending counsel told the judge that he objected to the line of questioning as it appeared to him that the prosecutor was badgering his own witness. The judge agreed and asked the counsel to reframe his question.

"You swore under oath that you would tell the truth, but it seems you are not willing to do so," the prosecutor said, looking disgusted. "I no longer have any further questions for this witness, but I reserve the right to ask her back for more questioning if required."

Elsie looked downcast as she stepped out of the witness box, and as she slowly walked back to her seat, she tried to avoid the hostile stares from members of the public.

The prosecution then proceeded to call the officer who interviewed the victim as well as the doctors and nurses who examined and treated the victim at the hospital. To the judge's surprise, the defence did not raise any objection, nor did he seem interested in cross-examining any of the witnesses. Then the prosecution requested that they play the victim's pre-recorded audio interview to the court and jury.

The audio was not edited or doctored in any way, and it described in gory detail the years of abuse suffered by the victim. Being prompted in the interview, which was held at the hospital in the presence of Mrs Pearce, Child A told the police how Elsie Doland would abuse her verbally and never intervened on her behalf even though she had told her on multiple occasions about what was happening.

During the interview, the victim spoke of how her father told her never to tell anyone about their special relationship, and that even if she did, no one would believe her because everyone knew that children like her lied to get attention. She told them how terrified she was when the accused threatened to make sure that something terrible happened to her if she said a word. So, even though she wanted to tell her school teacher, she couldn't because she was afraid her father would kill her.

There was a palpable gasp from some of the jurors and members of the public, and when a female juror started crying, Judge Horace had no choice but to stop proceedings. He retired to his chambers and asked to meet with the two counsels and members of the jury immediately.

The judge sat and watched them file into his chambers and waited for the last person to close the door.

"Ladies and gentlemen, thanks to the outburst by a member of the jury, the case has been compromised and, as it stands, we cannot continue with the same constituted jury. Therefore, with immediate effect, we will begin the process of selecting a new jury panel."

Having said that, he dismissed them from his chambers and stomped out of the room, looking visibly angry. The jury members were all bemused by the judge's reaction to what seemed a normal expression of emotion by one of them, but some were silently relieved they had been dismissed. They already hated the case, they disliked the accused, were irritated with the way his mother fawned over him, and most of all, they were intimidated by the very four walls of the Old Bailey. It felt like a prison, and they could hardly wait to get off the premises. As they walked out of the chambers, the court clerk led them to where to sign off and collect their allowance for the time already spent.

This time no future date was set for the hearing. As everyone stood up to leave the courtroom and Michael was escorted in handcuffs back to the prison van, there seemed to be a brief altercation between Lady Donna and John Kimberley. For no reason whatsoever, the old woman walked over to where the Kimberleys were seated and let loose.

"All the lies you have woven against my son, and my family will soon be exposed, and everyone will see you for who you really are."
"Excuse me, Lady Donna…" Josie's father began.
"Pleeeease, don't talk to me," she grunted, glaring at him like a venomous snake.
"My lady, not here," Mr Quinn pleaded, holding her arm.
"This is not the place nor the time for such confrontation,

especially with the press waiting outside like hawks ready to pounce."

While all this was going on, Jennifer and Winifred noticed their father sitting alone in the same spot he had sat in all through the hearing. Knowing what he must be going through, they both went over to comfort him.

"Dad, are you alright?" Winifred asked, placing her hand in his.
Sir Ian did not respond, his gaze was fixed on his wife.

Over the years, one would have thought he would have gotten used to her behaving in such a manner, but watching her attack the Kimberleys and then squabbling with the lawyer made him realise that it was something he could never get used to.

"Dad," Jennifer nudged her father as if to say, "We're still here."

Sir Ian looked at his daughters and made to stand up, almost falling in the process. So, Jennifer and Winifred helped their father up and escorted him out of the courtroom. By this time, Lady Donna had already exited the room, and contrary to the rules of the court was on her way to speak to the press. Luckily, Mr Quinn just about managed to dissuade her. The woman's uncontrollable behaviour was getting a bit too much for Mr Quinn to handle and for a split second, he had second thoughts about representing Michael Doland. But being a proud man and a crowd-pleaser, he knew it was too late to back down. It would leave his reputation in tatters.

Even though Mr Quinn had his doubts about his client's innocence, his job was to win at all costs, and that was precisely what he planned to do.

22
Miss Peggy Jones
(Part 1)

F our weeks went by before the new jurors were selected and vetted for the case of R v Michael Doland.

The notice for the hearing had been posted on the court board, and both the prosecution and counsel for the defence were duly notified. Also, at the discretion of the Lord Chief Justice of England and Wales, Patrick Wallis, the case had once again been assigned to Judge Declan Horace.

Even though it was almost a month after the case had been adjourned, it still attracted massive public interest as clips of Leah's audio interview were regularly played on the TV and over the radio. The harrowing experience and trauma that led to her fleeing home had given the public an insight into the accused sexual culture. Now Michael Doland was being seen as a predator, a paedophile, a brutal animal! So, on the first day of the new hearing, Court 12 was packed; there were no spare seats available.

The defence had hired two more distinguished solicitors, whose briefcases were bulging at the seams. The prosecution, on the other hand, looked quietly confident. They believed they had a watertight case. So, it was merely a matter for the new constituted members of the jury to listen to the evidence and come to a conclusion. Easier said than done!

After all the protocols had been observed, Judge Horace got proceedings underway without wasting time on the preambles. His only admonition for the jury was they should not show any personal emotion or disclose details of the case to anyone. The judge also made it clear that if this was not adhered to, he would not hesitate to have the case adjourned again. Then he called on the prosecution to begin their presentation.

Without any controversy, the prosecuting counsel called on Angela Kimberley, Josie's mum.

"For the records, can you tell the court your name and your relationship with the victim."
"My name is Angela Kimberley. The victim is my daughter's child, and therefore, my granddaughter."
"Is your daughter married?"
"No, she is not."
"Can you tell the court the circumstances of the victim's birth."

Immediately the counsel for the defence put in an objection, contending that the opposing counsel was in error.

"Mr Quinn, what exactly are you objecting to?" the judge asked, a hint of irritation in his voice.
"My lord, I object to counsel asking a layperson how a child is conceived. That is not relevant to the case at hand."

The objection was lame, and it attracted a quiet and subdued hiss from the public gallery.

"Overruled," Judge Horace's voice echoed with an air of finality, and the prosecutor continued with his line of questioning.

"My daughter Josie was raped at the age of sixteen. The victim is the offspring of that abuse."

This time around, there was no outburst from the public or the jurors.

The Prosecuting counsel went on to ask Angela about her knowledge of the events and what led to the victim living with the accused. As he led her in evidence, she explained how the accused and his mother had come to the hospital and forcefully taken the child away from Josie while she was incapacitated. Angela's eyes were red with unshed tears as she remembered how helpless Josie had appeared while in the hospital, and how they were unable to stop the Dolands from taking little Leah away.

"I have no more questions for the witness," said the prosecutor before taking his seat.

The time had come for the defence to cross-examine the witness, and one could feel the tension go up a notch.

Mr Quinn was a big man; his size was something he used to unnerve witnesses. Taking his time, he slowly stood up, and for about fifteen seconds, looked straight into Angela's eyes, but she didn't flinch. Angela had been briefed about his antics, and she was ready for whatever he threw her way. Finally, the defence counsel approached the witness stand.

"You are Mrs Angela Kimberley, the alleged victim's grandmother, yes?" he began.
"Yes, I am."
"You have told this court that the alleged victim was the

product of rape, yes?"

"Yes," Angela replied, not sure where his line of questioning was leading to.

"In addition, you told the court that your daughter is also a rape victim, correct?"

"I believe I did."

"Please, Mrs Kimberley, a simple yes or no will suffice."

"Yes, and yes again," Angela replied sarcastically.

"Mrs Kimberley, there is no need to be sarcastic. I am only doing my job.

"Now then, how would you describe yourself; a mother who brought up her daughter well or one who allowed her daughter, at a tender age, to run...?"

"Objection my lord," the prosecutor rose to object to the badgering of his witness and to clarify, just in case the opposing counsel had not realised, that Mrs Kimberley's daughter was not the one in the dock, neither was she the one on trial.

"Sustained," the judge replied firmly. "The defence will refrain from asking irrelevant questions.

"My lord, I have no more questions for the witness at this time, but reserve the right to recall her if the need arises," Mr Quinn declared.

Angela almost tripped as she stepped out of the witness box, and if not for the prompt reaction from the court clerk, it might have ended up being even more embarrassing. Mr Goldberg was right; no matter how ready you think you are, nothing can actually prepare you for a real cross-examination experience. She now knew first-hand how terrifying it could be.

Angela composed herself and glared at Michael Doland and his lawyer as she walked back to her seat.

"How dare that obnoxious man question her about how she brought up her children," She thought, as she sat down. Angela was fuming, and if not for the clerk who just happened to offer her a glass of water at the time, she may have lost the plot. Deep down inside, Angela was grateful to God that little Leah would not have to go through this.

As she sipped her glass of water, Angela heard the prosecutor call out his next witness. She almost choked. No one had told her that Peggy would be giving evidence for the prosecution, and from what she could see, the defending counsel was none the wiser. He looked stunned.

"What happened? I thought she was our star witness?" Mr Quinn questioned the solicitor beside him.
"My thoughts exactly," the man replied.
"My lord," Mr Quinn began, "May we approach the bench?"
"You may, but it had better be relevant," Judge Horace declared.

As they stood before the judge, Mr Quinn cleared his throat.

"My lord, the person who the prosecution has called happens to be our primary witness, and therefore, I do not see how she can serve the opposing side."
"Well, the way I see it, it doesn't really matter if she is your main witness or not. You have every right to cross-examine her as you please," the judge replied, and with that, he dismissed the defending counsel's objection.

"You may proceed."
"Thank you, my lord. The prosecution calls Miss Peggy Jones."
"For the records, can you please state your name, and your relationship to the victim."
"My name is Peggy Jones, and I attended St Magdalene Girls school, the same school as the victim's mother. We were both

in the same class."

"So, how would you describe the character of the victim's mother?"

"Objection my lord. How can the counsel lead the witness to make a character formation for someone he himself said is not on trial."

"Sustained," the judge agreed.

"Alright Miss Jones, of your own volition, you went to the police to report a matter. Can you please tell the court what happened."

Peggy looked like a frightened rabbit. Head down and refusing doggedly to look at Michael and Lady Donna so as not to crumble with fear. She cleared her throat, but when she opened her mouth to speak, nothing came out. To her surprise, when she looked up, she saw her parents seated in the centre of the courtroom. They were looking straight at her, but the look on their faces wasn't at all encouraging.

Everyone in the courtroom waited anxiously for Peggy to say something.

"Miss Jones, are you alright?" Judge Horace asked.

"Yes, my lord, I am fine. I'm just not used to facing such large crowds," she answered nervously.

"Well, I know it can be quite intimidating, but take your time."

"Thank you, Sir."

She cleared her throat again and boldly began to address the court. She spoke about how she was envious of the victim's mother and subsequent events that led to her being involved in the case. Peggy confessed to approaching the accused and his mother offering to testify against Josie. She told the court how Lady Donna had given her money in exchange for her giving a misrepresented testimony under oath.

Peggy then explained how, when her conscience began to prick her, she decided to return the money to the Dolands. However, when they refused to accept it, she handed it over to the police and reported herself. That was when she decided to turn state's evidence.

As Peggy testified, she made no effort to exonerate herself in any way, and by the time she finished speaking, she looked drained of strength and emotion.

Judge Horace looked at the clock on the courtroom wall and proceeded to adjourn the case for the following day when Peggy's cross-examination would begin.

The court emptied very quickly with the press scrambling to get their reports into the evening news.
Peggy ran over to her parents, hugged her mum and wept on her shoulders. Then they left without stopping to talk to anyone.

On the other hand, the Kimberleys and Mrs Pearce were pretty pleased with how the day had gone.

"I could see the consternation and frustration in your eyes during your session with Mr Quinn, especially when he tried to insinuate your neglect in bringing us up," Bruce laughed at his mum as they walked down the steps.
"Well, I was not about to sit there while he tried to impugn Josie's character. Can you imagine the cheek of that man!"
"Mum, that's what lawyers like him are paid to do. I still think defence lawyers are given more leeway during cross-examination though. I guess that is because their client's life is at stake."
"I thought Peggy really did well despite the intimidation," said Mrs Pearce. "It must have been a very harrowing

experience for her."

"Yes, I actually felt very sorry for her," Josie said.

Bruce had seen Peggy and her parents leave in a hurry immediately after the hearing was adjourned. He knew that the next day was not going to be easy for her as the counsel for the defence would seek to demolish and discredit her evidence and make her out to be an unreliable witness. He also feared that they might charge her with perjury.

Bruce decided that he would call Peggy, later on, to let her know that he was really proud of her and to encourage her to stay strong when facing Mr Quinn's onslaught.

23
Miss Peggy Jones
(Part II)

The day before, Peggy had spoken confidently and precisely as she testified as a prosecution witness. Today, as she took the stand, she faced the defending counsel's cross-examination.

Mr Quinn was under no illusion about the lack of sympathy the public felt for his client, but all he needed to do to turn this around was convince the jury. Should he go for the jugular and prove Peggy Jones to be of unreliable and dishonest character, or should he surreptitiously undermine her evidence? Like it or not, Peggy was a pivotal witness to both the prosecution and the defence.

At first, Peggy appeared nervous, but then she seemed to remember the conversation she had with her parents and Bruce's late-night call. No matter the badgering that was sure to come from the defence team, she was going to stay strong.

"Your name is Miss Peggy Jones, and you stated in your sworn affidavit, which I present before the court as one of the exhibits, that you attended the same school and were in the same class as the mother of the alleged victim, is that so?"
"Yes," Peggy stated confidently.

"And in the sworn affidavit, you also stated that you and the mother of the alleged victim were not the best of friends for some obvious reasons. Do you mind telling the court what those obvious reasons were?"

There was an immediate objection from the prosecuting counsel.

"We have stated over and over again that the mother of the alleged victim is not on trial and therefore, Miss Jones' opinion on their relationship is simply irrelevant."
"Mr Quinn, is this question of any relevance to the case at hand?" the judge asked.
"Yes, my lord. It is our intention to show to the court that our client is not the monster he is being made out to be," Mr Quinn replied.
"The objection is overruled with a caution noted. Miss Jones, you may answer the question."
"Yes I swore an affidavit to that statement," Peggy stated as she looked at Bruce and Josie. Then she refused to answer any further questions even though Mr Quinn glared at her with open hostility.
"My lord, it seems Miss Jones here is not willing to corroborate the affidavit which she swore to. I would, therefore, ask the court to declare her a hostile witness."

Justice Declan Horace fixed a fatherly gaze on Peggy.

"Miss Jones, you are not here as a suspect, but you are required to answer questions that are relevant to this case," he said in a tone intended to put her at ease. "Your cooperation is vital to this case, but if you do not cooperate, you will be held in contempt of court. Do you understand?"
"Yes sir, I understand," Peggy replied, her voice audibly shaking. "However, I decided that I would no longer give evidence for the defence because when I swore that affidavit, I was not told that I would be called up in court as a witness.

I also acted out of spite, malice and envy towards the victim's mother, something I now regret."

"Why did you act maliciously towards the victim's mother?" the judge asked.

"I am so sorry, sir," Peggy broke down in the witness stand. "Josie, please forgive me. It sounds silly now, but I was jealous because you were liked by everyone in the school. By agreeing to testify against you, I felt that for once in my life, the limelight would be on me."

As Peggy continued to cry profusely, Judge Horace called for a one-hour recess, asking the court to resume at three o'clock that afternoon.

The court reconvened at three, and with Peggy once again taking the stand, Mr Quinn, speaking in a deceptively mild tone, continued to focus on the content of the witness' sworn affidavit.

"I put it to you, Miss Jones, that you knew exactly what you were doing when you swore that affidavit."

"No sir, I did not. Neither did you explain it to me at the time," she countered, staring at him angrily.

Mr Quinn then proceeded to grill her on her inconsistent accounts of what transpired when giving evidence for the prosecution. He implied that she was not just a liar, but also a gold digger because she demanded to be paid by the Dolands.

"That is not true, and by the way, I did not ask for a dime. You were there when Lady Donna offered to pay me for my services and naively…"

"No, Miss Jones, you were not naive at all. In fact, one could claim that you actually wanted my client, the accused, all to yourself."

Before the prosecutor could object, Judge Horace reprimanded Mr Quinn and warned him to desist from deliberately attacking the witness.

"Mr Quinn, if you are insinuating that I have taken a fancy to Michael Doland then I can only conclude that you are confused and deluded. It doesn't take a genius to see that the accused is not a nice person," Peggy responded to the surprise of the judge.

"Miss Jones, you have not been called to assess the character of the accused," Judge Horace said with a stern tone. Then turning to the jurors, he told them to disregard the witness' last statement.

"I am very sorry, my lord," Peggy responded.

All she wanted was for this cross-examination nightmare to end. She could feel the tears welling up in her eyes, but was determined not to breakdown in the presence of Mr Quinn and the Dolands. She was not going to give them the satisfaction of watching her fall to pieces in the courtroom.

Mr Quinn went on to ask why she had not gone to the police earlier to expunge her affidavit implying that Peggy knew that they would not believe her. He then went on to say that the only reason why she had offered to testify for the prosecution was for the simple reason that she hoped they would protect her.

Peggy replied, saying that, at the time, she was undecided as to what to do next and the reason why she approached the prosecution was simply because she knew that they would accept the truth. She also told the court that she had returned the money to put her conscience at rest. But Mr Quinn was like a dog with a bone, annoyingly persistent.

"But I put it to you, Miss Jones, that you returned the money only because you felt the amount was not enough, and what you could not obtain through fraud, you were willing to acquire by blackmailing my client."

"That is not true," Peggy yelled angrily. "You are making all this up to discredit me because I refused to give evidence that would exonerate your client."

The defending counsel seemed buoyed by Peggy's reaction and delved even deeper by suggesting that the Kimberleys had paid the witness more, hence the change of heart.

Now, Peggy was no longer upset, she was annoyed.

"That is a lie, and you know it," she countered. "If I was actually influenced and motivated by financial gain, then I would be on your side."

For the first time, Mr Quinn looked frustrated. He was beginning to realise that the witness was more stubborn than he had envisaged. She wasn't going to budge. So, in desperation, he moved the motion to hold Miss Jones in contempt of court as he alleged she was perverting the course of justice.

Justice Horace appeared to be in a quandary. He wanted to be fair and impartial to both parties, but at the same time he was tilting towards believing her confession; that Peggy's initial motive to testify against the alleged victim's mother was borne out of naivety and childishness. Declan actually admired her gumption, how she stood her ground while giving evidence and took the blame for her actions which led to her deciding not to be the defence's star witness. So, using his discretion, he overruled Mr Quinn's motion.

With time far spent, Judge Horace adjourned the case until the next day.

24
Breaking Point

Sir Ian decided that it was time he and the family had a serious discussion about Michael's trial. So, he sent for his two daughters, Winifred and Jennifer, and their husbands.

He had thought about doing this sooner but felt that as the case was already in court, then maybe he should allow the legal process to take its course. However, that day as he sat in the courtroom, he had a rethink.

The trial was beginning to take its toll on everyone. Tempers were wearing thin; the lawyers on both sides were getting frustrated and impatient, undermining witnesses over legal issues was becoming a lot more frequent, there were altercations between members of the press, and it had recently come to Sir Ian's notice that Judge Declan Horace's wife had developed a sudden illness, and two members of the jury had been hospitalised. Also, as the trial was taking a lot longer than expected, it was starting to have negative financial implications on the Doland pocket.

As the family gathered that night, Sir Ian thanked everyone for coming over at such short notice despite their busy schedules, then wasted little time in telling them why he had called the meeting.

"You see, I am not as strong as I once used to be, and Michael's case is taking its toll on my health. Now, your mother might not admit it, but even she is beginning to slow down."

Sir Ian slowly looked at each member of his family, from his wife to his daughters and their husbands.

"Jennifer, do you remember our discussion before the trial? I said it would be better for your brother to simply plead guilty, and maybe we could procure a doctor to assess Michael's mental state. Remember?"

Jennifer nodded. Sir Ian continued.

"Well, as usual, your mother blindly stood by her son and disagreed with me. You see, I knew the trial would take longer than everyone thought it would, and it wasn't that hard to foresee the hostility it might attract from the public and ultimately the jury. Why? Firstly because the victim is a child, secondly because the victim was Michael's daughter, a little girl entrusted into his care, and dare I say, the offspring of another one of Michael's victims. The shame this case and the trial has brought upon our family cannot be quantified."

There was absolute silence as Sir Ian spoke. Everyone, except Lady Donna, listened not just out of respect, but because they wanted him to air what was in his mind.

"Since the second week of the trial, I have not been to the club. Do you know why? Because I was shunned by my friends and contemporaries. It was a traumatic experience for me. One that will be difficult to recover from."

He took a sip of his tea while they all waited for him to continue. Sir Ian took his time.

"Apart from all that, our finances have been dealt a heavy blow. Thanks to hiring three lawyers along with other expenses, I have to tell you that we are struggling."

Unsurprisingly, this caught Lady Donna's attention.

"Ian, are you implying that we should fire these top lawyers and engage the services of mediocre ones, for our only son?"
"Donna, can you please let me finish for once?"
"No, I refuse to listen to what you are insinuating. Not at a time when the case is going so well, and there is even the likelihood of an acquittal. We can't give up now, the stakes are too high," Lady Donna said, glaring at everyone like a crazy woman.
"Mother, please sit down," Winifred began.
"Young lady, don't you dare patronise me! I will no longer tolerate your sniggering. Your only brother is in jail with all kinds of criminals and without proper care. Only God knows the kind of food they feed him in those cells. Oh, Michael, my one and only son!" She started sobbing.

Winifred's husband gently pulled his mother in law back to her seat and gave her a box of tissues.

"Listen to yourself, Donna. Do you actually believe that Michael will be acquitted?" Sir Ian shook his head in disbelief. "You have no idea the gravity of what is at stake. Your son's violent, incestuous behaviour is not only a grave crime but one that is abhorred by society at large, anywhere in the world."
"So dad, what do you suggest we do, because as you just hinted, there is every likelihood the jury will find him guilty?" Jennifer asked.

"No, not my son," her mother shouted. "Over my dead body! We have the best lawyers in the land and if that is not good enough then maybe we should offer some sort of gift to those involved with Michael's case. We need to do everything we can to avoid an impediment in the outcome of the case."

"So, in other words, you want us to try and bribe the judge and jurors to secure a not guilty verdict for your precious son?" Sir Ian asked, looking at his wife as if she had lost the plot. "Are you so blind that you have not noticed that the members of the jury have already made up their minds? Remember, I was on the bench for years. Trust me, I know the signs. Our son is guilty, and they know it."

Sir Ian was right.

"Jennifer, you asked me what we should do next," he continued. "The day little Leah was found at the train station by that lady, was the same day she was interviewed by the Sexual Offences Investigative Techniques Officer in the presence of the social worker. All this was recorded. I remember her saying that Michael reeked of alcohol each time he came into her room to abuse her, which could imply that he knew exactly what he wanted to do, but needed to be under the influence of alcohol to do it. I don't think there is any way out for your brother.

I would suggest we urge him to do a plea bargain with the court. It is not too late for him to admit his crime, but time is not on his side. I can tell you where the case is going, I have seen it all before."

Lady Donna jumped out of her seat and stomped out of the room without so much as a backward glance at her family.

"Little Leah mentioned that she and Frances shared a bedroom, but when Leah turned five, Michael moved Frances to another room to give him easy access to her," Winifred's voice shook emotionally. "Poor thing, and to imagine that Michael did all this under the same roof as his wife, Elsie. I just find it so difficult to understand and forgive."

Winifred's husband took his wife's hand as he tried to calm her down.

"Winny, my dear daughter," her father began. "I once read an investigator's chilling but true perspective on cases of sexual abuse. He spoke about how domestic violence and rape are closely related, and that a man who commits rape will more than likely commit domestic violence. They almost go hand in hand. If you are willing to slap a woman like your brother has done to Elsie for years, then you are willing to rape a woman. It is just another form of abuse."

"But Dad, are you saying that Elsie has always been afraid of Michael and that he abused her both emotionally and physically? I guess that's why she started drinking, but that wasn't the answer to the problem," Jennifer declared.

All the while, both sons in law had not uttered a word preferring to listen unless called upon to say something. That was their default stance whenever they found themselves in a Doland family meeting, especially if their mother in law was there. But with Lady Donna out of the room, Richard, Jennifer's husband, had a few things to say.

"I agree with you, sir. We all remember what Michael tried to do to our little girl. The fear our daughter experienced on that day has turned her into an introvert who is afraid of men. At times I even think she is afraid of me. It has been a trying period for my family, and we are still going through counselling, hoping she will soon overcome this fear. All I can say is if someone could persuade Michael to just swallow his pride and plead guilty, it would spare the family from further embarrassment."

But as Richard spoke, they all knew it was a waste of time because without Lady Donna's cooperation that was never going to happen.

Winifred decided to go in search of her mother and saw her driving out of the house without saying a word to any of them. For a brief moment, she stood rooted to the spot, not knowing what to do. Then she brought out her phone and called her mother. Surprisingly, Lady Donna answered almost immediately.

"Mother, where are you off to? You know we all came over to try and sort things out. At least, out of courtesy, you should have told us where you were going."

"Winny, I am very disappointed in you, but you never cease to amaze me. Did you lot actually expect me to sit there while you castigated your only brother, judging him even though he has not been found guilty of any crime? What happened to innocent until proven guilty?" she shouted at her daughter.

"But this is different, and..."

"How is it different?" Lady Donna interrupted. "What do you know about being unsure of your only son's future?"

"But mother, that is exactly why we need to talk about it, to get a mitigated sentence for Michael. I just don't understand why you can't show the same sympathy to that little child. After all, you were the one who orchestrated her removal from the Kimberleys while her mother was still in the hospital!"

With those last words, Winifred dropped the phone and returned to tell the others about her heated exchange with her mother.

Afterwards, Richard, who was now becoming rather vocal, decided to bring the social media's interest in the case to everyone's attention. He told them how social media users, especially on Twitter, had expressed horror at the way witnesses, especially Peggy, were being interrogated, and how the bullying tactics engaged by the defence lawyers, especially Mr Quinn, had added to the online rage. The hashtag *#LeavePeggyAlone* was trending, and some went to the extent of starting a fundraising page to raise money partly so they could send flowers and other gifts to Peggy, but mostly to help sheltered homes that housed domestic and sexually abused women and children.

"Well," Sir Ian began, "let us pray that there will be no surprises from your mother."
"Dad, what do you mean by surprises?" Jennifer asked.
"You know your mother, only heaven knows where she is right now, but I can assure you that she is up to no good."

The entire family, except Lady Donna, had concluded that the case was a lost cause from day one. Jennifer and Winifred had always been against going to court. They wanted their brother to confess and spare the family from weeks of torture, but thanks to their mother, their plea fell on deaf ears.

It was almost eleven o'clock at night when they all got up to leave, and as Sir Ian saw them off, his wife drove into the compound. Not wanting to speak to her, the girls and their husbands hurriedly said good night to their father and left.

25
Anxious Wait

The trial was finally drawing to a close, and there was great anticipation and anxiety in the Kimberley household because, even though the case seemed like an open and shut one, no one could predict what the outcome would be. They were under no illusion regarding Michael's guilt. The question was, would he be found guilty on all counts, and if he was, what would the sentence be?

Josie found herself replaying her cross-examination by Mr Quinn when she took the stand. He tried to make it look like she was the accused, insinuating that she lied to her parents and the police. He then tried to impugn her reputation by suggesting that she had a boyfriend before the attack and that she was sexually active. Josie knew Mr Goldberg had warned her about how ferocious and intimidating the defence counsel would be, but she had not expected such an onslaught on her character.

The prosecution immediately raised an objection to the bullying of their witness, but Josie was more than willing to give an account of how Leah came into being, how she was raped by the same

Michael Doland.

By the time the defence realised their mistake, it was too late. The public gallery erupted once again; they clapped their hands and chanted, "Shame, shame, shame," in the direction of the defence.

Judge Horace immediately requested for order in the court before threatening to remove everyone from the public gallery if such behaviour repeated itself.

As all this rushed through Josie's mind, she heard a ping on her phone. Josie was pleasantly surprised to see that it was Bosede facetiming her.

"Hi BA, how are you?"
"I'm fine. We just landed at Heathrow."
"Oh, wow! Fantastic. Did you say 'we'?. Who did you come with?"
"Well, I'm here with my fiancé, my parents and Tope. Remember I told you that we would try and make the closing of the trial. Well, here we are!"
"Thank you so much. I really appreciate it. So, where are you guys staying?"
"We're all staying at dad's apartment in Mill Hill, apart from my fiancé who is going to his sister's place in Edmonton."
"I can't wait to see you, auntie Kathy and uncle Chris, and even that comedian of a brother of yours. I'm also really looking forward to meeting your knight in shining armour," Josie laughed.

Bosede told Josie how they followed the trial on the BBC World Service, as well as over the internet, and thanks to the snippets of information that Mr Kimberley had shared with her dad, they were up to speed with the latest happenings.

Finally, they both did a little facetime wave and promised to meet up at the Old Bailey later that morning.

Josie waltzed into her mum's room and told her about the Archibong's arrival. All of a sudden, there was a spring in her step. She was very fond of the Archibongs; they had been so good to her and helped set her on the road to recovery. Josie could never forget how Mr Archibong had asked Dominic Parkes, the current Metropolitan Police Commissioner, to pursue both cases. The rest as far as she was concerned was history.

Her mind went back to when she was led in evidence by the Prosecutor. She described what she went through after being raped, some of which she never revealed until that day. Josie narrated to the court how she feared being infected with HIV since, in her young mind, she thought all rape victims automatically contacted the virus.

Josie told them how on several occasions she had wanted to commit suicide but somehow, because of her faith in God and her belief that one day she would get justice, she managed to pick herself up and bided her time for a day such as this when she would confront her attacker in a court of law. She testified how as a result of what happened, she found herself distrusting and sometimes hating members of the opposite sex. Josie went on to tell the court how in rebellion, she fled to Nigeria, and how a country she had no knowledge of had practically changed her life.

For over thirty minutes, Josie related her emotional ordeal. It got to a stage that she was weeping so much that the judge had to tell her to stop and catch a breath, and when he asked if she would prefer to continue the following day, Josie declined vehemently. There was no way she was going to let Michael Doland and that mother of his think she was a weakling.

Having spoken to Bosede, then looking outside to see the clear blue sky, Josie felt like the sun had risen upon her. "It is going to be a good day," she thought to herself and smiled as she hummed the tune to her favourite song, "Oh what a beautiful morning" from the musical, Oklahoma!

The Kimberleys had planned to make it to the court early to avoid the press, but to their consternation, aware that both counsels would be making their closing submissions to the jury, they were already camped outside the Old Bailey, and there was no avoiding them.

As soon as the family alighted from their taxi, there was a frenzy of activity as reporters rushed towards them.

"Miss Kimberley, what do you expect will happen today?" one reporter asked, sticking his microphone in Josie's face. "Do you think…,"

Out of nowhere, Mr Salmon Goldberg appeared.

"Excuse me, please," he said in his booming baritone.

He shoved the reporter to one side and ushered the family up the stairs into the building.

Even though Josie had already told BA where they would be, the Kimberleys were still surprised to see the Archibongs so soon. The joy of seeing each other was evident as there were smiles and hugs all around.

"Now you must be the famous Josie," Benson, Bosede's fiancé, said with a wide smile.
"And you must be the one and only Benson Fiberesima, aka Fibs," Josie said, looking at BA before bursting into laughter.

"Well, there's only one person who calls me that. So, I guess that confirms that you truly are Bosede's best friend," Benson replied.

Josie blushed.

"Well, it's good to see everyone. Now the only person missing is Mrs Pearce. Do you still remember her, the lady who rescued Leah from the train station?" Josie asked, looking curiously at Mr and Mrs Archibong.

"Of course we do," Kathleen replied. "And, how is Leah by the way?"

"She is fine; a happy and well adjusted young lady considering everything she has been through. She still lives with Mrs Pearce and her daughter, but we should get the custody hearing rolling once the trial is over. If all the submissions are settled on time, then you should get to see her before the weekend."

They walked into the courtroom and took their seats. The room was charged with expectation and uncertainty, and Josie especially was beginning to feel a bit anxious. Chris Archibong, who was sitting beside Josie, gently squeezed her hand encouragingly and smiled.

"It's going to be fine, Josie," he said.

"Thank you, Uncle Chris," Josie replied, smiling nervously.

The public gallery and press section overflowed with curious observers as the jury was ushered in. Moments later, the prison guards escorted in the cuffed Michael Doland. He was wearing a grey and powder blue suit with a red tie and a crisp, white shirt. Michael shook the hands of his defence team with bravado as if to show that he was confident the verdict would go his way.

Bosede looked over at where the Dolands were seated and immediately fixed her gaze on the frail, elderly man with silverish grey hair. "That must be Sir Ian," she thought. She was right. Josie had told her that Sir Ian had served on the bench at the Family Division of the Royal Courts of Justice for more than twenty years, and it was easy to see. Even though he had a resigned, distant look in his eyes, there was still that air of dignity and authority about him. For some reason, she felt sorry for him. Bosede suspected that for someone who had been in and out of courts almost all his life, this was the last place he wanted to be right now.

The atmosphere in the court was getting tense, the restiveness was beginning to affect the lawyers on both sides. Most eyes kept looking at the two clocks on the courtroom wall, and many wondered when Judge Declan Horace would make his entrance so that the day's trial could commence.

Thirty minutes went by, then one hour, and still, there was no sign of the judge. Suddenly the clerk entered the room, and after a brief word with both counsels, they both got up and followed the clerk into the judge's chamber.

On entering the chamber, they were surprised to see the judge talking to two young teenagers. Mr Quinn immediately recognised them; Michael Jr and Dora May, his client's children. He wondered what they were doing there.

The judge asked both lawyers to take a seat. Then after assuring his two young guests that he had noted everything they told him, Judge Horace politely asked them to wait outside.

Once the children shut the door behind them, the judge looked at both men and shook his head.

"I would like you to listen to this," he said, and he played the audio recording of what the two children said about their father.

Even though Michael Jr seemed more vociferous in condemning his father, calling him all sorts of names, it was obvious that both siblings shared the same view about their father.

"But my Lord, how did they get into your chamber?" Mr Quinn asked, looking confused.

"Don't ask me, I have no idea. All I know is that the children were waiting here when I entered. The clerk said he saw them lurking surreptitiously around when he arrived in the morning. So, I guess they must have sneaked in when he turned his back," the judge replied. "Anyway, I am not asking you to analyse what they said, but I do want you to be aware of what Michael's children think of their father."

"But we do know that this cannot be used as evidence?" the prosecuting counsel quipped, looking at the judge as if he had lost all sense of court etiquette.

"Gentlemen, I am sure you will agree that this is an unusual case, and I hope that there will be no more surprises," the judge concluded as he seemed to ignore the prosecutor's concerns.

With that, he left his chamber for the courtroom, followed by the two counsels.

26
Closing Statements
(Part 1)

So, almost two months after the trial had begun in Court 12 at the Old Bailey, the prosecuting counsel, Ms Camila Teddington QC rose to give her closing statement to the jury.

"The defendant, in this case, Mr Michael Doland, is alleged to have raped and sexually abused Child A, his own daughter, who was conceived when her biological mother was also raped by the same man. He is also alleged to have tried to cover up his sordid, incestuous act by giving the police misleading statements and evading arrest for over six months.

From the evidence, and from what we have witnessed all through this trial, I submit to you that the defendant has not shown any remorse whatsoever for the damage and harm he has done to the young child placed in his care.

What chance did Child A have against a big, strong individual like the defendant? The defence claim that Child A knowingly allowed herself to be in the wrong place at the wrong time and now regrets it. But a five-year-old, sleeping in her bedroom at night; would you classify that as the wrong place at the wrong time? The truth is the defendant abused and destroyed the trust that Child A had in him, the man she called father.

He stealthily, knowing precisely what he was doing, set out to commit the systemic sexual assault of Child A from the time he arranged for his other daughter to move out of the room she shared with her, giving him unbridled access to the bedroom and Child A."

Addressing the case of the defence that almost imputed that Child A was interested in what the accused was doing to her, the prosecution pointed out that a five-year-old child who had been made to believe that no one would believe her and then threatened with death would naturally keep quiet because she feared for her life.

She reminded the jury that, on several occasions, Child A did report the abuse she was being subjected to to the woman who she thought was her mother, but that woman simply ignored Child A's complaints.

Ms Teddington noted that if Child A was indeed a silly girl who made up a pack of lies against the defendant, then where and how did she sustain the injuries to her internal organs and the bruises on her body? He pointed to the medical and forensic exhibits that had been shown to the court.

"Michael Doland has pleaded not guilty to perverting the course of justice and withholding information relating to the incident, and he has consistently refused to admit he committed this heinous crime. But, from the evidence we have seen, and what we have heard in this courtroom, it is clear that Child A is not a liar, she simply told the inconceivable truth."

On the criticism the defence raised about Child A's interview with the police, Ms Teddington told the jurors that they must guard against assumptions on how they would expect a child of such a tender age to behave under harrowing circumstances.

The prosecuting counsel asked a rhetorical question of what the defence had alluded to regarding the delay between Child A running away and reporting to the police. To the prosecution, this was irrelevant.

"What we should be asking ourselves is why she ran away in the first place. At the time, in her childish mind, anywhere was preferable to the hell she was going through at home, in the hands of one who should have protected her. So, why did she run away from home? Child A ran away because she could no longer bear the pain and misery, she ran because she feared for her life. Child A ran away from home because she had no choice!"

Addressing the point the defence made about Child A not telling her teachers in school, or even the police, about what she was going through at home, Ms Teddington asked, "How many five to seven-year-olds report such things to those in authority, especially if they are being threatened? That's a child for you!"

Counsel praised Child A for her brave account of the horror she had been through and told the jury that as far as the prosecution was concerned, there were no inconsistencies in Child A's account of what had happened to her between the age of five and seven. She contended that even if there had been any inconsistencies, they were dealing with a child who had been traumatised by the abuse she had been subjected to. It was therefore unreasonable to expect anyone, young or old, having been through such trauma to remember every detail.

"Good schooling, a good upbringing and a wealthy home

counted for nothing when used to disguise the realities of an overbearing and shameless individual who did not care about the consequences of his actions towards a child in his care, who incidentally was an offspring of his own flawed character. The defendant knew he was hurting his child, but didn't care. He was only interested in gratifying his libido, albeit with a little child, his own child for that matter. We should not coat what this man is with fine words, but call him what he is. In my opinion, the defendant is a paedophile who preys on vulnerable young children.

The defendant's mother described her son as exemplary, wonderful, and one who loved all his children equally without prejudice. After what you have witnessed during this trial, would you use the words exemplary, wonderful and loving to describe the defendant? I leave that for you to decide."

In closing, Ms Teddington invited the jury, which consisted of seven men and five women to find the accused guilty.

As usual, time flew by, but before adjourning the court until Monday the following week, Judge Declan Horace turned to the jury and reminded them about the need to keep an open mind.

27
Closing Statements
(Part II)

O n Monday morning, the court reconvened once again, to hear the closing statement of the defence counsel.

An unbiased observer would have noticed certain things about the demeanour and bearing of the counsel. He came across as aggressive, often attacking the credibility of reliable sources and frequently making snide and sneering inferences in his conduct towards the prosecuting witnesses. He often asked the witnesses the same questions repeatedly and then manipulated their words to frustrate the prosecution. It seemed, and maybe rightly so that the only thing on his mind was to either get his client acquitted or, if that failed, go for extreme mitigation in the sentencing.

Mr Charles Quinn began his concluding statement to the jury.

"The burden of proof against my client lies with the prosecution. They must be able to prove beyond a reasonable doubt that the defendant is guilty. However, from everything we have witnessed over the past five weeks, this does not seem to be the case."

Mr Quinn suggested that the prosecution's case was not only flawed but laden with lies and innuendos and that they had tried to use morals and sympathy to blind the jury. He implied that the mind of Child A had been manipulated to make his client look like a monster and child molester, and took the pain to remind the jury that there was no DNA evidence to prove that his client had actually sexually assaulted his daughter. There was a stir in the public gallery as it seemed like the defending counsel had conveniently forgotten that when Mrs Pearce took Leah to the hospital, the forensic scientists extracted some of the defendant's DNA from the child's body which was even established as an exhibit at the beginning of the case.

He went on to mock the evidence given by the prosecution witnesses, especially Peggy's and Josie's and accused the police of tampering with the evidence. He also rejected the questions raised by the prosecution about Child A being intimidated by death threats issued by his client, calling them, "fabricated nonsense".

In an attempt to undermine Child A and discredit her audio statement, the defence regularly used humour and semantics to belittle and mock the victim, something which the jury found to be highly condescending and obnoxious. According to Mr Quinn, the investigation into the allegations made by Child A during her interview was virtually non-existent, therefore making her statement, to a large extent, null and void.

Most of the time, Mr Quinn offered no specific refutation of the facts of the case or the allegations made, beyond the denials of the defendant. He maintained that his client was a reliable witness irrespective of all the alleged lies he was credited with and that in this case, his client was the one telling the truth. Also, coming from such a respectable family and one whose father was on the bench for almost two decades, stood his client in good stead and therefore should make the jury's task easy.

Finally, directing his remarks towards the jury, Mr Quinn brought his statement to a close in his usual brazen way.

"Morals, emotion, sympathy, condemnation and personal judgment, should not be your guiding principles nor even considered in the trial of my client. The defendant does not claim to be a saint, but in this case, his only crime was to try and give Child A an upbringing in a comfortable home alongside his other children. My client's account of what happened to Child A which he willingly provided to the police, as well as the evidence of good character given by his mother proves his innocence.

This trial has been laden with inconsistencies and lies against the defendant, but through it all, my client has consistently maintained his innocence. You must, therefore, be convinced of the defendant's guilt before you even consider convicting him. If you are sure, then there should be no hesitation in your duty to convict, but if there is even a hint of doubt in your mind, then you must acquit. My client's innocence or guilt must not be based on the credibility or age of the victim. This case must be decided solely on the evidence you have heard in this courtroom which proves that Michael Doland did not rape his daughter. I, therefore, urge you to do justice and acquit the defendant."

The prosecution barrister, Camila Teddington QC took about five minutes to resubmit her conclusion to the jury, reminding them that the victim was a child whose protector had turned out to be her abuser. She told them how Child A would most likely never know the true meaning of living a normal life and how her relationship with the opposite sex would forever be tainted because of the actions of the defendant; a selfish, untrustworthy brute.

Finally, it was time for the presiding judge to give his submission.

Judge Declan Horace told the jury that any sexual allegation, whether it involved a child or an adult, would arouse a great deal of emotion and it was their responsibility to guard against prejudice or sympathy. He charged the jury to ignore press reports and comments about the trial on social media, especially the posts on Twitter that had recently grabbed the headlines. Judge Horace reminded the panel that all eyes were on them to come to the right conclusion based on their understanding and interpretation of the evidence given during the trial.

In his charge, Judge Horace told the jury that manipulation, control and revenge according to the defence were at the centre of the trial. While the prosecution claimed that this was not the case, the defendant alleged that it was and told the court that the whole process of coming to court was instigated by the victim's mother.

> "When you consider the issues raised about revenge and instigation by Child A's mother, you must be able to draw the distinction between what Child A said happened to her and a mother's desire to bring the perpetrator to justice."

Judge Horace instructed that, while they may have their own personal opinion about the sexual assault on the victim by someone she considered and called her father and protector, the jury should not lose sight of all that transpired over a two-year period in a young child's life as evidenced in her statement given to the investigating police officer in the presence of Mrs Caroline Pearce.

> "I hereby direct the jury to come to a common-sense conclusion, not based on speculation, but the evidence presented during this trial. If you are firmly convinced that the defendant is guilty, then you must find him guilty. If on the other hand, you think there is a real possibility he is not, then you must give him the benefit of the doubt and

find him not guilty. At the same time, if you are not sure, then you must find him not guilty. You must be sure of guilt before finding the defendant guilty.

I shall not ask you to deliberate today as time is far spent. The court will adjourn until ten o'clock tomorrow morning. In the meantime, as you have been told repeatedly, it is imperative that you do not discuss this case with anyone, including each other until you have come back into the courtroom tomorrow morning. You will then be ushered to the jury room to deliberate. So, to be clear, all deliberations will take place tomorrow and will be carried out when you are all together in the jury room.

I must also remind you that the evidence is now closed and you must deliberate and decide solely on the evidence and the arguments that you have seen and heard in this court. You must not do any work on the case until you start your deliberations together tomorrow morning. This simply means that there must be no private study, no taking of notes, and certainly no communication with the outside world," Judge Horace concluded.

28
Justified

That Tuesday morning, the court filled up quickly just like the day before. The court was told to stand as once again Judge Horace made his way in. As soon as he had taken his seat, the jurors were ushered back into the courtroom, and after being briefed, they retreated to the jury room for deliberations.

They were gone for just under two hours when the elected jury foreperson signalled to the jury keeper that they had reached their verdict.

For one last time, the jury was ushered back into the courtroom.

"Will the jury foreperson please stand? Has the jury reached a unanimous verdict?" Judge Horace asked.
"Yes, we have," he replied.
"How do you find the defendant?"
"On all ten counts of Rape, we the jury find the defendant Michael Doland guilty.
On all ten counts of False Imprisonment, we the jury, find

the defendant Michael Doland guilty.

On all four counts of Assault, we the jury, find the defendant Michael Doland guilty.

On all three counts of Breach of Trust, we the jury, find the defendant Michael Doland guilty.

On all five counts of incest, we the jury, find the defendant Michael Doland guilty."

As soon as the foreperson read out the verdict confirming that the jury had found the defendant guilty on all counts, the court erupted with cheers and clapping with some even taking the opportunity to make catcalls.

The judge immediately called for order, and when the noise persisted, he asked the court security guards to clear the public gallery as it seemed like the only way to restore order to the court.

The foreperson handed the verdict form to the court clerk, who in turn gave it to the judge. Judge Declan Horace thanked the jurors for all the work they had done during the trial before discharging them.

The judge had come prepared for whatever verdict the jury returned and was therefore ready to pass sentence on the defendant. So, after a one hour recess, Judge Declan Horace sentenced the defendant, Michael Doland thus:

"You have been found guilty on all the charges presented by the prosecution. You were given ample opportunity to plead guilty, which may have mitigated your sentencing, but you chose not to for reasons best known to you.

You have been found to have abused the trust that the victim had in you as her biological father. You continuously and systematically sustained your attack on an innocent and defenceless child who depended and looked up to you.

During the course of this trial, you have been shown to have subjected Child A to a barrage of intimidation and coercion. You knew exactly what you were doing from the day you moved your other daughter out of the room she previously shared with the victim, and as if that was not enough, you also removed the locks to the room, showing that your actions were premeditated.

For someone guilty of such a horrendous crime, you have not shown any remorse whatsoever during the trial. Instead, you have consistently exhibited what I would call an 'I don't care' attitude. The public, especially young people, must be protected from people like you. You are a danger to the female gender, both young and old.

Taking all this into consideration, I hereby sentence you, Michael Doland, to life imprisonment of which you will serve at least twenty years before becoming eligible, if at all, for parole."

With that pronouncement, Judge Declan Horace got up and exited the courtroom.

The press section of the courtroom erupted. There was a flurry of activity as they scrambled to notify their respective channels and networks of the verdict of a trial that had gripped the entire nation for the most part of two months.

As the counsel for the prosecution, Ms Camila Teddington QC and her team, gathered their files, the Kimberleys walked over to thank the team for helping to finally put Michael Doland where he belonged, behind bars!

"We were only doing our job," Ms Teddington replied, the smile on her face showing that she was extremely pleased with the verdict the judge and jury had handed down.

She also praised Josie and her family for their doggedness in seeing the case to its final conclusion despite the intimidation, pressure and threats from the defendant and his counsel.

Josie looked at her dad and smiled.

> "Dad, for the first time, I can actually say that both Leah and I have been justified."

A cuffed Michael Doland glanced over at where his parents were seated, but before he could say a word, he was whisked out of the courtroom by the two prison guards into the prison van that brought him to court earlier on.

Lady Donna looked on in shock, and Sir Ian was worried on her behalf.

> "Donna, it's all over. Justice has been served. It is time to go home."
> "Don't you dare touch me," she hissed at him angrily, jerking her arm out of her husband's hand.

Lady Donna gathered her coat and bag, and without saying a word to her celebrity lawyer and his team, flounced out of the courtroom. She was fuming wondering what could have gone wrong. She concluded that there had been a conspiracy against her son and even blamed the defence counsel for a lacklustre representation.

In her mind, she had already started planning how she was going to appeal on the basis that there was a total miscarriage of justice as the judge's direction to the jury was flawed and therefore erred in law. As far as Lady Donna was concerned, her son was a victim of the court's ineptitude, and the jury was made up of plebiscites who did not understand the rudiments of court proceedings and evidence.

"Lying bunch of hypocrites," she whispered bitterly under her breath.

She was going to prove to all of them that her son was innocent, especially that spineless old man who called himself her husband and could not even stand up for their son.

By the time the taxi dropped her at her home, Lady Donna had worked herself into a frenzy, so much so that she refused to eat. She walked straight past the butler, stomped up the stairs and into her room, slamming the door shut before locking it.

As she paced up and down, Lady Donna decided that she was going to visit her personal lawyer. She planned to change her will and leave all she had to Michael's youngest daughter, Frances, as she was the only one who hadn't betrayed the family.

After gradually calming down, Lady Donna took a couple of sleeping pills and washed them down with a shot of brandy, but even though she was exhausted, sleep eluded her. She lay down on her bed and tossed from side to side.

By nine o'clock the following morning, with less than an hour of proper sleep, Lady Donna was up and dressed. First, she planned to see her lawyer, after which she would visit Michael at the Wormwood Scrubs Prison.

The night before, she heard her husband calling her name as he knocked on the bedroom door, but she ignored him. So, with her taxi waiting outside the house, she slowly crept down the staircase, hoping to leave the house unnoticed. Unfortunately, her husband was in the kitchen having breakfast, but there was no way she was going to say a word to that traitor. So, she picked up her phone and pretended to be on a call. Sir Ian tried to catch her attention and even offered her a cup of coffee and some toast on a tray, but she just walked past him as if he wasn't there.

As she made her way towards the front door, she tripped and fell facedown, hitting the side of her head on the mantelpiece in the hallway. Her fall and scream attracted the attention of Sir Ian and the butler who came running to see what had happened.

"Oh my God," Sir Ian shouted, bending over his wife. "Quick, call an ambulance," he told the butler.

Sir Ian checked his wife's pulse and confirmed she was breathing, but they didn't try to move her so as not to cause further damage. Sir Ian noticed a trickle of blood coming from a gash on his wife's forehead and asked the butler, once he had called the ambulance, to get him some warm water and a cloth.

The paramedics arrived within fifteen minutes and carried out the necessary triage before attempting to lift her onto the stretcher. While they stabilised the blood flow and made sure she was comfortable, the paramedics also asked her what had happened. Even though Lady Donna was conscious, for some reason she couldn't speak, so Sir Ian told them the little he knew. Finally, they rolled her into the ambulance. Initially, Sir Ian offered to follow them to the hospital in Paddington, but when Lady Donna shook her head profusely, the paramedics advised that maybe that wasn't a good idea. So, Sir Ian told the butler to go with her instead.

As the ambulance sped away, Sir Ian called his daughter Jennifer and told her what had happened to her mother.

"I know you hardly see eye to eye nowadays, but can you and Winifred please go and see your mother immediately," Sir Ian told Jennifer.
"But Dad, where are you? Didn't you follow mum to the

hospital?" Jennifer asked, sounding a bit concerned.

"Well, I offered to, but you know your mother, she made it pretty clear that she didn't want me there. So, I had to ask the butler to jump into the ambulance and keep me updated."

There was a brief silence.

"Okay, I'll start making my way to the hospital now. I will pick Winny up on my way.

" Thank you so much, my dear." Sir Ian dropped the phone.

Jennifer and Winifred arrived at the hospital in Paddington within forty minutes and were on their way to the Accident and Emergency ward when the butler called to inform them that Lady Donna had unexpectedly slipped into a coma and had been rushed to the Intensive Care Unit. The sisters looked at each other, shocked into silence and hurriedly made their way to the Intensive Care Unit.

As they sat down outside the ward, Jennifer and Winifred remembered the hostility their mum had shown them after the trial, but right now, the past was forgotten and forgiven; after all, she was the only mother they had, and she needed them. How were they going to tell their father about his wife's current condition? They were still in a state of indecision when the attending emergency doctor, who they met when they got to the ward, approached them. Winifred immediately noticed from the doctor's countenance that something was wrong. She was right.

"I am very sorry, but your mum has passed away," he said in a solemn voice.

The grief in their eyes said it all. Eventually, with great difficulty, the sisters thanked the doctor and went inside the room to see their mother.

When they came out, they, along with the butler who they had told to switch off his phone so he couldn't talk to their father, drove straight to the family house. Sir Ian was in the living room, still in his pyjamas when they walked in. From the look on their faces, he suspected the worst and almost fainted but for the prompt action of his daughters, who quickly ran to his side. There was no way they were going to lose both parents on the same day.

"She was in such a hurry to leave. There was a taxi waiting outside the house so I can only assume that she had an important appointment with someone", Sir Ian said in a quiet, subdued voice. "I even urged her to have some breakfast, having learnt from the butler that she did not eat anything when she came back from court yesterday evening."

Jennifer and Winifred knew that their mother must have been up to something, but now they would never know what. The other thing they couldn't understand was what made their mother slip. They went to the hallway to see if they could find what caused the fall, but there was nothing visibly obvious. So, they surmised that maybe she was feeling dizzy having not eaten since returning after the trial the day before.

Sir Ian and his daughters were still coming to terms with Lady Donna's death when the police and the crime scene investigators arrived. They had been notified as the incident occurred at home. The forensic investigators inspected the mantelpiece on which she supposedly struck her head and took photographs of the area where she fell, while the police interviewed Sir Ian and the butler, who were the only ones at home when the accident occurred.

The police left about an hour later promising to get back to the Dolands after a preliminary investigation into the accident had been completed, but assured the family that they were satisfied that it was an accident and there was no foul play involved.

News of Lady Donna's death made the headlines of the evening papers. It was also aired on the radio and widely televised. The news filtered through the walls of the HM Prison Wormwood Scrubs and finally into the prison cell where her son was serving time. When Michael finally got his hands on the evening newspaper, he read how his mother had fallen into a coma and died in the hospital, after accidentally falling at home.

The news was too much for Michael to bear. After receiving his sentence the day before he had thought about how to end his life, but now that the only person who cared for and believed in him was gone, Michael felt there was nothing left for him to live for.

He waited till nightfall and silently barricaded his cell door with his bed. Then he took his bedsheet and made a noose around his neck, propped himself up on the chair and tied the sheet around the overhead pipe. Finally, he kicked away the chair underfoot.

Michael Doland died of strangulation that night, but his body was not discovered until late the following morning when he didn't show up for the roll call, and his food was still untouched by the door.

29
Almost Over

The Kimberleys were shocked when they heard about the deaths of Lady Donna and her son Michael, and their sympathy went out to Sir Ian and his daughters, who would have to live with the pain of these unfolding horrors.

Josie could only imagine what Jennifer, who she had grown to know and like during the course of the trial, was going through. She was tempted to call her but decided against it as it was only appropriate to allow the family time to grieve their loved ones privately. Josie, therefore, concluded that she would call Jennifer and offer her condolences over the weekend.

On that Thursday night, the Kimberleys held a little get together to celebrate their victory in the Michael Doland case. For the first time, Leah would spend the night with Josie in the Kimberley household. It was like a prelude to Josie having full custody of Leah, and both mother and daughter could hardly hide their excitement.

Apart from Leah, the Kimberleys were also hosting the Archibongs as well as Mrs Pearce and her daughter Emily. Bruce had taken the opportunity to invite Peggy too, who had slowly but surely been accepted by the Kimberleys as Bruce's girlfriend.

After all the guests had arrived, Josie asked if she could say a prayer for the Doland family. John and Angela looked at each other and smiled. They were pleasantly surprised. The thought had actually crossed their minds, but considering everything their daughter had been through with the Dolands, their main concern was the way she might react if they brought it up. However, listening to Josie's heartfelt words put their fears to rest.

When Josie finished there was a resounding "Amen" from everyone, and after a brief silence the celebrations began. Angela had spent most of the day in the kitchen cooking up a storm with Daphne and Lois and judging by the looks on faces, and how everyone kept going back for more, it wasn't in vain. It was a sumptuous and very delicious meal, and they all ate and drank to their heart's content.

Even though they tried to avoid it, the sudden death of Lady Donna and Michael's suicide inevitably made its way into the night's discussions, and they all wondered what would become of Michael's children.

"It's such a shame because they are such lovely children. So well mannered," said Carol.

"Yes, they are, and they love Leah so much," Josie replied, looking very whimsical.

"Do you know what the prosecutor told me after the sentencing?" John Kimberley started. "He said that Michael Jr and Dora May somehow had managed to sneak into the judge's chamber on the last day of the trial."

"Really!" Josie exclaimed.

"Yes, really," John nodded. "Not only that, but they also told the judge that their dad was a nasty man, and because of what he did to their sister Leah, and their mum, he deserved to go to jail for a very, very long time. In fact, I was told that Michael Jr actually told the judge that he hated his dad and never wanted to see him again."

"Are you serious?" Chris Archibong asked.

"I'm not kidding," John replied. "The truth is, the only person who testified and vouched for Michael's character was his mother."

As the night drew to a close, John ordered a taxi to take the Archibongs to their apartment in Mill Hill.

Chris and Kathleen Archibong, along with their son Tope, planned to visit their daughter and her family in Aberdeen over the weekend. However, what made the trip all the more exciting was that Margaret and Emmanuel had recently given birth to twins, Kathleen and Chris' first grandchildren.

Bosede was staying in London with her fiancé to do some shopping for their wedding, which was just four months away. Unsurprisingly, the Kimberleys had been invited for the wedding, but due to prior engagements, it was looking like Josie and Bruce would be the only ones representing the family.

Even though a date had not yet been set, Josie had already started preparing for her daughter's custody case, and the words that Judge Declan Horace used as he sentenced Michael Doland still rang clearly in her head.

"I am seriously concerned that the defendant Michael Doland will persist in his evil ways," he said. "Judging by the unrepentant attitude he has shown through the course of this trial, I am led to believe that he will, more likely than not, be a substantial threat to the society for the unforeseeable future. Therefore, in my judgement, it would be in the society's best interest to keep Michael Doland as far away as possible from women and children to ensure that they are not harmed in any way at the hands of the defendant."

These words filled Josie with confidence and belief that Leah would soon be back where she belonged; with her!

Also, now more than ever, she knew what her mission in life was. Josie was tired of reading and hearing stories about paedophiles, incest, repeat rape offenders, and men who derived joy from physically abusing women. It made her blood boil. But she was determined to take a stand, determined never to give up. Josie was going to fight for justice on behalf of abused and rape victims, and to help with this, she planned to set up centres for women and young adult advocacy.

Epilogue

A year after the death of Michael Doland, Josie Kimberley was granted custody of Leah without opposition from any quarter.

She bought a run-down building in north-west London and with the money she inherited from her grandparents and a small loan from the bank, she refurbished it, after which Josie moved out of her parent's place and into the newly renovated house with Leah.

As the building stood on a substantial piece of land, Josie also decided to kick start her dream by laying the foundation of her sheltered accommodation for young, abused girls. Having already registered her outfit, JOSEAR Shelters and Advisory Centre, a name that significantly amalgamated hers and Leah's as Josie saw both of them as the first victims to occupy the shelter, she formed a Board of Directors made up of herself, her brother Bruce, and Kathleen Archibong.

Two years went by, and on a bright, sunny spring day in the month of April, the JOSEAR Shelters and Advisory Centre was officially declared open. Two days later, they admitted three vulnerable teenagers who had been groomed and abused as sex slaves.

Josie Kimberley currently works and liaises with other high-profile rape victims; lobbying members of parliament in an attempt to change the legislation regarding how the Police and courts handle rape cases; to ensure that victims are not intimidated or made out to be liars before their voices are actually heard.

So far, they have managed to persuade the lawmakers to carry out the first reading of the Victim Protection and Impartial Evidence bill in the House of Commons. Even though their proposal was met with considerable opposition from some members, the group of advocates for the change were assured that the bill would be pencilled in for another mention in later sittings.

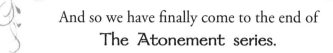

And so we have finally come to the end of
The Atonement series.

I simply cannot thank God enough for
the special grace He has given me to enjoy this
amazing experience of fulfilling this long-held dream of mine.
I know that the inspiration to write each of these books
could only have come from You!

To my family and friends:
Knowing that I can always count on you means so much to me.
Thank you for your prayers, your care,
your never-ending love and for always being there for me.
I appreciate you all.

And to every reader who has been on this breathtaking journey
with me; taking in every word and supporting me with encouraging
words. Thank you so, so much!
My prayer is that the words in these books will leave
an indelible mark on your hearts and truly make a difference.

So, till we meet again through the pages of my next book,
Stay safe and remember,...

...it is never too late to follow your dream!

– Stella Jackson –

About
The Author

Stella Jackson is the founder of Martha & Mary Ministries, a charity established to support orphans, widows and the elderly in today's challenging world. She strongly believes that everyone, without exception, deserves a second chance and through this charity continually helps the disadvantaged fulfil their destinies.

Stella is a happily married mother and a proud grandmother.

Other Books By
Stella Jackson

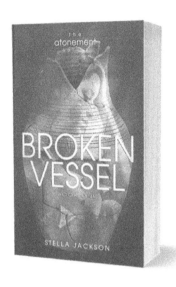